STAGE BY STAGE

My thanks to Catrin Barnes and
Imogen Pinchess for their help and patience

STAGE BY STAGE

or

A Spiral

"i"

Griff a Gwen

David Rees

ISBNs
Paperback: 978-1-80541-289-2
eBook: 978-1-80541-290-8

Just a few weeks ago, I was browsing in Waterstones bookshop in Canary Wharf, trying to find a suitable birthday present for my great-nephew who had moved to live in Stratford. As I was perusing the shelves, I came across a jewel of a little book - "I've Lived In East London For 86 ½ Years" - about Joseph Markovitch. This is not what I finally settled on as a gift for Henry since I wanted something related to Stratford, in the past, present and future, but Joseph Markovitch was a gift from me to me. From Canary Wharf, I returned home for a light lunch and on to a siesta with my gift of the book by Joseph which I did not close until I had finished reading through to the end. I think it was the key that opened the story of my own little journey in life. After all, most of us have a story which can be related to others who might be interested in discovering that they too have a tale to tell.

PART 1

My story begins with me popping into this world in Liverpool in the mid-1930s. I have little recollection of this, but I gathered later in life from my mother that she hardly knew of my arrival. So, my impact seems to have been minimal, unlike the extremely difficult births of my twin brother and sister, who were older by seven years. What I do remember was a pair of slippers with rabbit heads and flapping ears at the front and white undercoated tails on the heels. I still recall how my mother would bring my supper upstairs, sometimes with beetroot sandwiches, delicately cut. Often, she would read me some poetry, of her choice of course, and naturally, I cannot remember the poems and failed in life to ask if she could remember them. As she would read, one hand would stroke my head with her fingers gently running through my hair until she had lulled me to sleep, and so, she was supposedly freed from the responsibility of this child for the night.

So, how did my parents first meet and what were their origins? My father was an absolute Welshman with roots from south Cardiganshire in Southwest Wales, between Cardigan and Carmarthen, and north Pembrokeshire where Welsh was the language. My "mam-gu" (grandmother/nain) could not speak or write English, or so it was claimed. She referred to the English as Saeson, pronounced "saison", similar to the Scottish word "Sassenach". The Welsh are a distinctive people in their own right and one of the many branches of Celts. The Celts who are probably the most closely connected are the Welsh, the Cornish and the Bretons, and they are also the nearest in language. There are several Cornish and Welsh words that are the same and Breton is close too.

My mam-gu was one of twin girls, daughters of a bailiff for Bronwydd, the local estate belonging to the manor house of the squire, Sir Martyn Lloyd, a baronet claiming Norman descendancy. Mam-gu and family lived in one of three estate cottages in Aber-banc, a hamlet on the edge of the estate, and generation after generation of her family had worked there. She and the lady of the manor had a pact that my father must be educated. So, he spent much of his time at the big house. Lady Martyn Lloyd seemed to treat my father as something of a surrogate son. There was an heir to the estate, but it seems he was an addicted gambler and spendthrift who squandered the whole estate. Later, after the son was killed in the Great War, the estate had to be mortgaged. This way of life was still basically feudal, or rather, in the death throes of feudalism across the whole country. It reached its demise with the end of the Great War. Tragically, some years later, Bronwydd subsequently "died" too. I have happy memories of the place during my early childhood evacuation but, in my adulthood, they remain romantic though tinged with a sadness of things past.

Both my parents were born before the end of Queen Victoria's reign and lived through the reigns of five monarchs - Victoria, Edward VII, George V, Edward VIII, George VI and Elizabeth II. My father went to the nearest grammar school where he advanced brilliantly, especially in mathematics and science. He went on to study at the University of Wales in Aberystwyth and from there, at the age of twenty-two, enlisted in the Great War as an ordinary young Tommy in the Royal Medical Corps. He was one of those involved in the Battle of the Dardanelles and returned home only to be immediately dispatched off to Northern France, and indeed, the trenches. He was a stretcher-bearer and would have to advance to collect or transfer the dead and wounded. After many such sorties, wading through deathly blood and mud, he was shot and captured. Later, if he ever talked about this horror, which I only heard him do once, he praised the German surgery he was given. He was then transferred with other British prisoners to the Black Forest. Meanwhile, his family were notified that he had been reported missing.

Villagers would call at the cottage to commiserate with his mother who refused to accept the news and sent the commiserators on their way. Then the second telegram came to say that he was missing, believed dead. Again, the commiserators called and his mother sent them on their way because she said her Griffi would return. Finally, the third telegram came to say that he was dead. However, despite this message, his mother said to all that her Griffi would return. His sister Rachel recounted to my mother later that Rachel and her father, my Tad-cu (taid, grandfather), went to Henllan, the nearest village station, to collect him in the family trap pulled by Ned, the pony. She recalled how this thin, very pale and silent young man stepped off the tiny one-coach train. Yet Griffi still had his piercing blue eyes and vivid wavy red hair. Nobody spoke. His father handed him the reins and Ned's ears pricked up. Griffi stood up and jerked the reins gently and Ned trotted off merrily all the way home to Aber-banc. Griffi and Ned had a special relationship, or so the family said.

Slowly, Griffi's speech returned. Soon afterwards, my father went up to Lincoln College, Oxford to read Philosophy and Theology in which he gained a Double First. Whilst at Oxford, he met my mother, Gwen (Gwenfron). She had a cousin also at Lincoln who would invite her for the odd weekend. He was quite friendly with my father and that is how the two Gs met. Many years later, my mother described to me that the first sight of her future life partner was of this pale-skinned, brilliant red-haired young man with such blue eyes but oh, so silent. He let everybody else talk even though some had not served in the war, and some were pacifists. And father remained silent, but he seems to have found an instant ally and defender in Gwen.

And so, where did Gwen Morris come from? Birmingham. She was certainly second or even third-generation Birmingham, but originally from Flintshire, North-East Wales near Holywell. Her ancestors were stonemasons, and her Taid/grandfather was the stonemason in Birmingham who provided the stone for the building of the impressive Birmingham Town Hall and Civic buildings. He married Anne Salesbury a descendent of William Salesbury who, along with Bishop Morgan, translated the Bible (certainly the Old Testament and the Cranmer book of Common Prayer into Welsh) into the Welsh language following the Reformation and decreed by Henry the Eighth. Gwen's mother was Mary Evans from Corris in North Wales, famous for its slate quarries. Her own mother had died soon after her birth and so she was initially brought up by an innkeeper and his wife who lived somewhere in the area. Meanwhile, her father went off to the Klondike thinking he would make his fortune in the gold mines. However, that did not happen. (This seems to have been so on both sides of my family - money seems to have escaped us.) So, he, my great taid/grandfather, returned to Wales and soon remarried. Mary was returned to her new home and stepmother who seems to have been very kind and all-embracing of her stepdaughter. However, Mary took some time to settle into her new home. She went to the local school where the Welsh language was forbidden by the authorities. Often, they were caught and were smacked with a metal ruler or strap. Whilst she spoke Welsh in her home, she certainly mastered the English language.

Soon afterwards, aged fifteen, she left home and crossed into England and went into service in the Midlands, rising from teenage parlourmaid to housekeeper. We always knew her to be quite strict on table manners and correct on table setting. She was an excellent cook and good at general housekeeping. The lady of the house, knowing that Mary had been raised to go to the Nonconformist chapel every Sunday back home, would arrange for the family carriage to take her to the Welsh chapel in Suffolk Street in Birmingham. That is how she met John Morris, her future husband. In those days, the Church and chapel were a type of social centre, and this lasted certainly until post-World War II. In a modified way, they still act as such where people still have a faith.

Mary and John had two daughters, Gwenfron, shortened to Gwen, the elder, being born within a year of the parents' marriage. Her younger sister arrived nine years later. Being older, my mother developed her own independent interests. She particularly enjoyed going off to the Music Hall regularly and would drag along the younger sister who was less inclined towards such entertainment. However, tragedy struck the family during the early part of the Great War. Their father developed cancer of the pancreas, suffered greatly and died around 1916, leaving his widow aged just over forty without any pension as there was no Widow's Pension in those days. Gwen was the only breadwinner for the family of three. She was just about nineteen and was private secretary to the boss of Britannic Insurance who seems to have been very supportive of young Gwen. Soon afterwards, my Nain, Mary, was struck by the rampant "Spanish Flu" that had already led to many fatalities here and across Europe. In those days, there were no antibiotics or inoculations and it was uncertain whether my Nain would pull through. Meanwhile, the younger daughter, at the age of ten, was sent to her stepmother in Wales. I do not think it was a happy experience for her because, throughout her life, she never wished to speak about it. Strangely, my Nain spoke only English to her daughters and husband, though he learnt some basic Welsh with a noticeable English accent when he went to Wales as his mother-in-law would only speak Welsh.

Just a few years after my father left Oxford, my parents were engaged and there was an engagement party in the Birmingham home which just about all the Birmingham cousins attended - and there were many of them. Father was meeting them for the first time and no doubt it was a daunting experience. It seems he retired into his silence. But there was another young man equally silent among the cousins. These two young men were transfixed for who was this cousin, Jim Morris? He was the other stretcher-bearer retreating on the battlefield in Northern France. Two stretcher-bearers passing in the dead of night. When he returned home, Jim dispensed with religion but would always come to hear my father preach because he knew Griff would have no truck with cant.

Griff and Gwen married in 1924. From Oxford, Father had become the young minister and already distinctive preacher of a Welsh Presbyterian church in Holloway in the Tufnell Park area. They lived in a flat at the top of a large house in Bisham Gardens in Highgate with views across Waterlow Park to the tennis courts and on to the famous Highgate Cemetery. Often in our childhood, my mother would refer to trudging with shopping up the unending steep Highgate Hill from Archway. Four years later, the twins arrived in the Dick Whittington Hospital at the bottom of Highgate Hill. It was a very difficult birth and the twins remained in incubators for six months. In 1929, my father was invited to be the minister of the Welsh Presbyterian Church in Liverpool, in and known as Princes Road.

With Liverpool being such a vital port on the Atlantic, it was a very prosperous city – well, for some. And then I came along - I am not sure if by default. Well, I can claim I gave my mother an easy time.

Then war came and irreparably changed everything. So, we, my brother and sister and I were sent off, evacuated, to my father's homeland, set between Cardigan and Carmarthen and very close to the magical river Teifi, a river of salmon and coracles and several water-driven flannel mills. It was the first time the twins had been separated. Being the infant, I was sent with my sister to one aunt, my father's eldest sister, and my brother was sent to my father's middle sister, Rachel. Our parents remained in Liverpool for another year. Our aunts and cousins were completely Welsh-speaking, as are my younger cousins of today.

I do not recall experiencing any sadness from being separated from our parents. I was sent to the little primary school which stood behind our Aunt Mag's house. I remember absconding from school and dashing down a tiny pathway from a hole in the school wall back into my aunt's kitchen in time for her freshly made Welsh cakes, but I don't remember being scolded for it. Aunt Mag had one son, Cunedda, who was in the army, and three daughters - Eluned, who suffered from epilepsy, from which she later died, and whose attacks were really frightening, then Morfydd, who, at 18, was drafted into war munitions in South Wales, and Rhian, two years older than the twins, who was like my other big sister. Also, there was Clifford, the cousin, who had tuberculosis and had one leg amputated.

Both my aunts had goats, so, every morning, we had goat's milk at breakfast. They also both kept chickens. Sometimes, Aunt Mag would kill a chicken for the main meal of the day. I would be sitting in the main room and kitchen on the flagstones or on the sparse rag rugs dotted around, and it was not unusual for a dead chicken to run around even after having been strangled by Aunt Mag and had its head chopped off. Then there came the day of the pig killing in this hamlet. I never attended the pig killing but I could hear the animal's squawks and screams. Then the pig would be carved up into portions and loins. Several pieces would then be sold around and hung up from the living-room ceiling from meat hooks. I can see Aunt Mag slicing rashers of the bacon and frying them on the kitchen range. But it was such salty bacon that I hated it. What I did like was my aunt's "cawl", Welsh farm country soup made from leeks, onions, potatoes, carrots, slices of bacon and parsley - delicious. In those days, cawl was part of the staple diet in Wales for the country was poor, especially in the rural areas.

I have three recollections of death around that time. The first is of being taken around to visit two homes where the mam-gu of Vera, the local blacksmith's daughter, had died. I think Vera was John's girlfriend;

John was not backward in that area. In the old Welsh custom, the coffin was set on two chairs, one at either end, usually in front of the parlour window with the blind or curtains drawn until after the burial. I was quite unfazed by this early experience. After all, what could the aunts do with the child? He could not be left behind at home. Vera's mam-gu/grandmother was dressed in her Sunday black and had a broken front tooth between her lower lip and her chin. I did not think this was a nice idea.

The second deceased was similarly laid out, but she was really pretty and was all in white and had a smile, so she had to be an angel. Then there was the time of going up to Llangynllo churchyard to clean the family graves. This really was the Martyn Lloyds' family church, and, as my mam-gu's family was so connected with this great family, albeit in service, that is where nearly all my family are interred. It is a beautifully peaceful place to be, even if in transit. On this day of cleaning the graves, the aunts would bring a dixie can of tea and two cake tins filled with Welsh cakes and fruit cakes.

Similar arrangements would be made at harvesting time, especially for the rakers. In those days, these were the local women mostly, because the men were already in the war. And lastly, on New Year's Day, with everywhere covered in snow, we would put old stockings over our shoes so as not to slip. We would call at the cottages and exchange 'calennig' - a particular local word meaning New Year greetings. We were not given money but fruit or biscuits or cakes. I clearly remember climbing the long hill to Anni's round lodge beside the main gates to Bronwydd. She gave us her freshly baked biscuits and cakes, and on such a winter's morning, they were far more appreciated than pennies. In those days, and in the country especially, we had not hit the age of consumerism. To me, the biscuits were really as Proust describes the Madeleine biscuit. We were such hungry, healthy and happy children.

Soon, my father was to leave Liverpool for Wales. He was given a professorship of the Welsh Presbyterian Theological College in Bala, Y Coleg y Bala, really a finishing "shool", following earlier theological studies in Aberystwyth. Meanwhile, my mother remained in Liverpool for several months during the initial Nazi bombing. Liverpool was the main port for shipping across the Atlantic and, as such, was a special Nazi target. Once my mother arrived in Bala, we three children and cousin Eluned left Aber-banc and Henllan for Bala which became our home for the next fourteen years. Bala is famous for its lake, Llyn Tegid, named after a Welsh prince from distant times, and it is the largest natural lake in Wales. Llyn Tegid is famous for the fish "gwyniad", said to be found only in Bala and a lake in Hungary. I can vouch for the truth as I have seen the fish in a glass framed box in Bala. From the lake, the

River Dee begins to wind its way helping to create such beautiful scenery all the way to the Dee estuary at the apex of which Chester rests - by origin, Caer, a Roman fortress city - so separating England from Wales. Bala and its surroundings are some of the most beautiful landscapes for walking and mountain climbing.

Sadly, soon after our arrival, Eluned had a massive epileptic fit. Her mother was summoned to take her back home which meant a journey over the mountains and hills by car, in a basket chair covered in blankets. It was a very solemn send-off and she died very soon afterwards. I remember we three children and Mother picked masses of beautiful snowdrops and ivy from the college grounds, which were carpeted with them, and somehow or other, they reached Aberbanc in time for the funeral and burial in Llangynllo. My father, of course, took the carefully wrapped snowdrops in ivy as he would have been taking the funeral service. Soon after this, I was taken ill. I was placed on the carpet beside the coal and log fire in my father's study. I do recall writhing with the pain in my tummy. This turned out to be appendicitis which developed into peritonitis when the appendix burst. With no major hospital for such operations nearby, a car had to be hired to drive the sixty miles to Liverpool. According to my parents, Dr Bob said to the Bala driver, "Drive like bloody hell". Today, he would probably say something much stronger and more fiery. Thereafter, Dr Bob and his family became our family friends. So, I survived, even though the magic of penicillin and antibiotics had not quite reached us.

We lived in a wing of the college with three large reception rooms and two kitchens but with few domestic facilities, and indeed, those we had were primitive even for then. Half the house had electric lighting and certainly no heating other than fires for there was plenty of wood from the grounds around us. Coal was plentiful in those days as we benefited from the Welsh coal mines of the south and from around Wrexham towards the English/Welsh border. Upstairs, we had small paraffin stoves. Sometimes we would slip backwards whilst trying to warm ourselves and gain a burn on the bottom, and thereby, be stigmatised with a stinging red patch. We all had a stone hot bottle covered in mother's old stockings for our feet and hot water bottles filled with boiling water for the main part of the bed. I well remember chilblained toes!

We took on our respective little jobs which our mother said was also part of our war effort. The bathroom was ice cold most of the time and the very solid iron bath was, to me, huge. In such a large house, we were all able to have our own rooms. John, my brother and I shared the big bed in his large room at the top of the house until my mother discovered that he had plucked out my eyelashes. So, that was the end of us ever sharing a bed again. Perhaps my mother also found that John had been concealing a copy of Titbits under his pillow. She did not remove it so she must have had a kind heart. I remained at the top of the house in another quite large room. We all had our set night for a bath in rotation for it took so long to heat the water. During the war, throughout the whole country, the blacking out of all windows was compulsory. If any light leakages were seen and reported by the wardens, that would mean prosecution and being charged on the spot.

From evacuation, I soon settled into the change of rhythm of life in Bala. I was just over the age of five and often, quite early in the morning, I would jump into my sister Anne's bed for her to read from A. A. Milne's Winnie-the-Pooh and that is what encouraged my reading. Just a few years ago, having inherited Anne's Pooh collection, I re-read them with great joy, even after all these years, as my bedtime reading. Since reading had entered into my life, my father must have thought he would occupy me in the vast library of mainly theological and Welsh books. Initially, he opened up one of the libraries to secular journals and newspapers such as the Times, Literary Times, The Listener and other periodicals. Also, because of the Western Alliance with the Soviet Union, the Russians often released their propaganda periodicals to advertise their rich wheat harvests in the Ukraine and South Russia. Thus, Father would get me to stamp everything that entered this library using the stamp of the college. All three libraries became places of my own escape. There were vast shelves, some quite deep enough to take a small boy curled up in embryonic form, allowing me to continue reading my favourite book at the time. At the age of eleven, I can see myself in such a position reading Jane Eyre and crying over Jane's childhood friend Helen dying from tuberculosis.

The large room between the two main libraries had two vast wooden tables sandwiched together specifically for table tennis played by the students, which we three children commandeered during the students' vacations. I became really keen on this domestic sport and was really proud of myself when I beat the older twins.

Seeing repeats of Dad's Army on television, I am reminded of the Bala Home Guard, of which my father was the padre/chaplain, when, every week, he would don his uniform wearing the peaked cap which did not suit him. My mother would stand on the doorstep laughing at his strutting off to the town gathering. I never saw them on parade other than when gathering around the local War Memorial of the Great War (WW1). One day, there was high drama when the War Office in London issued a high alert that the Nazis planned a parachute landing on the west coast of Wales and concentrated on the Bala area because of its basin shape. So, the older men of the area, including my father, gathered together the family axes, saws, and any kind of bladed weapons and took them for sharpening to Mr Jones in Bron y Graig, the large house on the other side of the hill from The College. What the locals could have really achieved in such a happening I am not sure. I think it was before this alert that we few children who lived around the College were playing in the bushes and came across a young German parachutist tangled in the midst. I do not recall any alarm from us, though since she lived close by, I think it must have been Gaynor who ran to one of her parents who quickly alerted the local police station. Soon, impressive Inspector Davies arrived and took the young German away for the night. This probably saved his life for it was better to be a prisoner of war than be sent on to the Eastern front and either be killed by the Red Army or sent to a Gulag never to return to his homeland.

I was used to seeing German prisoners of war in their blue denim POW uniforms with a red circle on the back of the tunic. These young men were allocated to local farms and were well fed and looked after by the farmers. I remember I would see one man meeting his local girlfriend, one of the very few Catholics in Bala, as the young German was Catholic too. I later heard that he had stayed on and settled in Bala and that they had married and attended the Catholic mass in the first Catholic Church in Bala (or so I would imagine) at the back of the Blue Lion pub. There were also some Italian POWs allocated to other areas close to Bala. They wore brown uniforms with yellow circles on the back of the tunic.

The College was set on a hill a little out of the small town - or so it seemed to me. In the early years, most of my friends were from local homes. There was Gaynor Williams, two years older than me, then there was John Sogno, a boy of my age, who, with his mother and sister, had been evacuated from Eastbourne. Two sisters, Ann and Sally, had been evacuated from London due to the bombing and had moved into the big house on the other side of the hill from the College. They had come with their mother, Mrs Toogood, and their grandfather and stepmother. Mrs Toogood and my mother formed quite a close friendship. Ann and Sally went to the local Elementary school at the other end of the town towards Llyn Tegid, so we always walked there and home together, quite a walk for such youngsters. There was no other way. I still remember when little 5-year-old Sally announced on our way home on College Hill that I was her sweetheart and that later on, we would be married. Sadly, that was never to be.

Towards the end of the war, when there was a lull in the bombing, their dying grandfather decided that they must all return to London. After he died and whilst their mother, Mrs Toogood, was on night duty as an air warden, the V2s - Doodle Bugs - had already started savage attacks on London, and there was a direct hit on Buckingham Palace Mansions in Buckingham Palace

Road, Victoria, close to the station. The whole family were killed; grandmother, an aunt who was a nurse and off duty that night, little Ann and Sally. Mrs Toogood was the only survivor. When the news came through to my mother, she too was devastated.

Their uncle, their mother's brother, was the Welsh novelist Richard Llewelyn from the coal mining areas. He had written the smash hit novel 'How Green Was My Valley' about family life in the coal mining areas of South Wales. Later, it was a huge success as a film and my mother took me to see it, an outing which I remember still. The heroine, Angharad, becomes pregnant and is denounced in the local chapel. I remember that scene particularly and thought that the deacon who denounced her was the devil incarnate. In the film, Angharad - such a beautiful Welsh name if you can get your tongue around it - is played by the American/Irish film star Maureen O'Hara, which seems to have been a rather odd choice. There were many wet eyes coming out of the Victoria Hall/Neuadd y Buddig. This was where regular hops (dances) took place but mainly girls with girls and women with each other with handbags flying from their arms, as most of the men were in the war. Others, including farm lads, stood around gaping at the females dancing a stately or sometimes less stately waltz or quickstep, and an attempt at a foxtrot or slow foxtrot, but never an attempt at the tango - no men.

As a little boy of six or seven, I loved singing, especially "penillion". This is typical of the mountainous and hilly areas of Northwest Wales amongst farming traditions through the centuries. A group of singers would trek from one farm to another with the harp, a Celtic one in those early days, over the shoulder. The singing is mostly contrapuntal to what the harpist plays. I still see little Miss Jones seated at her harp. As children, we would be deeply concentrating, shoulder to shoulder, almost arm in arm, desperate to keep our tune and not get absorbed into the Welsh air Miss Jones was playing. We loved it and I am happy to say that Penillion-singing is still as strong as in my childhood, and far more exciting than tapping a mobile in the current era. I then went on to sing in children's choirs, all in Welsh and in various Eisteddfodau (Welsh song and verse festivals), both at local and national level. I remember competing as a boy soprano in Bala in the Victoria Hall to which my mother accompanied me. As I was singing, I spotted her sitting a few rows from the stage looking very nervous for me. I was not feeling nervous at all. I did get a prize but sadly, not the Gold/First.

There would be times when my mother had gathered enough clothing coupons to make a sortie to Liverpool for the big shop to clothe us three children. The twins were already away in boarding school, so Mother and I would be up at six in the pitch-black morning and walk to the local station to catch the one-coach train to Bala Junction and change to maybe a two-coach train to Ruabon that would take us to Birkenhead to catch the ferry across the Mersey to damaged and bombed Liverpool. I loved the ferry for there was something threatening and thrilling about it, especially the excitement when hearing the clanging of the ferry boat bell.

Then off we would go to the various big shops - George Henry Lees, Bon Marche, Henderson's, Lewis's, then Reece's for some lunch. Mother would have arranged to meet up in the stores with some of her old friends from her previous years in the city before moving to live in Bala. For her, it was a joy to leave the Welsh pastoral scene and come back to her urban scene. Then, after Reece's, we would be off to a matinee, often a Shakespeare at the Royal Court. I remember still quite vividly Wolfit's Shylock, and also Abraham Sofaer as Lear. On another visit, it would be a pantomime – 'Babes in the Wood' with Ethel Revnell and Gracie West. They rented the twin garage from my mother in the Liverpool days. Then we would rush to make the same journey in reverse to get back home. When questioned by my father why she would take me to the theatre, she would reply, "It is very important that the child should have the chance to go to the theatre and see these great actors". Mind you, we went because she wanted to as it was a furtherance of her love for going to Music Halls during her childhood in Birmingham.

There is no doubt it sowed some seeds for my love of the mystery of the theatre.

Back home in Bala, I remember making a maquette of a stage out of a cardboard box and an orange crate. Despite not being very technically minded, I managed to work out some tracking for the working of the house curtain. Out of her rag bag, my mother produced some ruby-coloured remains of an old velvet dress, and so it was. Then there was the matter of the audience. I gathered together my two teddy bears and rabbit and collected my sister Anne's collection of dolls, even the broken and headless ones; anything to fill the house. They were very obedient and silent, but, as I found out, they were bums on seats, a very appreciative audience. Once, when I was not around, my father had gone into my room and had seen all the mute little folk. He rushed to my mother to express his horror thinking I was playing with dolls! My attitude to these silent little folk was quite pragmatic. They were filling the "house".

Living in Bala, my greatest joy came from the wonderful walks along the lake, over the hills and up the mountains, often on my own. Sometime towards the end of the war, my parents gave me a full-sized bicycle. It was like a new release in my little life! It was very heavy and I had to put blocks on the pedals. At this earliest stage of having the iron horse, I would walk from home into the town to pitch myself by the statue of Tom Ellis, the famous Welsh educationalist in the nineteenth century. When nobody was around, I would climb onto the plinth of the statue and saddle my iron horse and ride off down the main street to the lake, Llyn Tegid. My target was to cycle the ten miles around without getting off! And I did it too. But boy, was I sore around the bum! I had such joy from my horse. My little world was my oyster. A memory that returns still is of many tastes, sights and sounds – in spring, lying under a grove of larch trees that were bursting with buds of amazing light green, matching perfectly with the green leaves of the surrounding bluebells.

My father was something of an enigma to many in Wales, yet he had his fans for his fine and direct preaching. During the war, a community of nuns were evacuated from Merseyside to a Welsh manor house in the Bala area, set up on a hill overlooking the lake. Somehow, my father had developed a connection with the Mother Superior and they would meet in the Blue Lion pub at the back of which space had been found for the start of a Catholic church – yes, in the midst of the seat of Calvinistic Methodism. It is obvious that my father and the Reverend Mother related intellectually and in aspects of spirituality and prayer. As an eight-year-old mite, he used to send me walking two or three miles to this community to collect books of prayers, including the Douai Book of Prayer. I was used to seeing the nuns shopping in town in their grey flannel pleated habits with dangling black beads, starched wimples and white woollen stockings in shiny black clogs. When I arrived at the convent, the nuns immediately took me into the kitchen for freshly baked biscuits. One of them would show me around the herb garden they had created. I even found my own way into their chapel without the nuns. Some of the local people of Bala found out about my visits to the nuns, so, the outcry in Welsh of some was: "What does Principal Rees think he is doing sending the child to those old Papists?". He was delighted when he heard of this little uproar. This did not deter him. Well, this was a long time ago and supposedly, ecumenicalism had not yet arrived, let alone future secularism.

One day, in the early hours, there was a horrific droning noise and an explosion. A plane had crashed into the farmyard of a remote farm way up in the hills beyond the College. I rushed out of bed and jumped on my iron steed along with other boys and reached the farm. There were bits and pieces of the plane scattered around the fields. Walking beside a hedgerow, I came across two airmen sitting quite upright, wide-eyed but in separate spots in the hedge. They were dead. I cannot remember anything else about the event.

I well remember when the Nazis were bombing London with the V2s, "Doodle Bugs", and Londoners, particularly from the East End, were being evacuated. One Sunday, they arrived in droves at little Bala station and this stream of evacuees/refugees, women and children, making their way to the College which had been designated as the reception centre. From there, many were collected by local folk who would billet them or accept them into their own homes. The remaining ones would stay overnight at the College. I think most of them felt so dislocated and hated being taken away from their homes, even despite the bombing. My brother John and I watched from his bedroom window at the top of the house, gazing at these tragic-looking wanderers through Father's marine telescope.

Soon afterwards came VE Day. A huge flag of the Welsh Dragon was hoisted from the tower of the college. John and Anne had returned for two nights from boarding school for the celebration of peace in Europe. Later in the summer, I was able to join my friend John Sogno in Eastbourne where he had returned home with his mother and sister once hostilities in Europe had stopped. It was beautiful summer weather and I remember still the heavily perfumed lavender hedgerows around the town. With the Hiroshima atomic bombing came VJ Day which of course was the most thrilling experience for everybody, seeing the people abandoning any sense of sobriety. Men & women young & old rushing into the sea fully clothed, drunk screaming, singing & dancing & sending fountains of sea water upwards.

One day, John and I were taken along the tops of the Seven Sisters to see Beachy Head, a favourite site still for suicides. I remember us both, on our tummies, moving to the very edge of the cliffs and looking down to the Channel. That truly was a very disconcerting sight which perhaps initiated my subsequent fear of heights. I think it is the hypnotic power of such heights that can derange a person, hence Beachy Head's magnetic draw for the suicidal.

Quite soon after the War - it must have been winter 1947 - the whole of the UK suffered one of the severest winters on record. The country was coping with great austerity through lack of resources and restrictions which the Labour Government was having to impose following the awfulness and shortages through the war years. Although in the rural areas we escaped the bombing, there were heavy food restrictions as dairy products, meat and vegetables were commandeered and sent off to the cities, and in the case of Bala, this was generally to Liverpool and Merseyside. Heating during this particular winter was a great problem as all means of transport were out of action, hence, no coal could get to the most needy and remote areas. Water pipes were completely frozen. I remember my father, stripped to the waist with a towel around his shoulders, running through the grounds to a stream with a little waterfall for a mini shower, shaving and cleaning teeth. Of course, I loved this situation. I had made my own sledge, helped by the College caretaker/gardener, who had found some steel runners to attach to the base. So, off I trudged in deep snow to the golf course that had a steep hill. Whizz, and off I went - the Conqueror! Returning after the slide back to the top of the hill was less exciting. Word came about that some coal was arriving in the station coal yard, so Papa took my sledge to get his supply. On his return, he spied a farmer he knew who offered to tow my little sledge with the supply of coal up the hill. Papa thought this was great because it would save him from having to struggle up the steep College Hill. However, to his dismay, when he reached the foot of the hill, there was the sledge with the sack of coal. Nonetheless, there was the coal - our gold.

It must have been the summer following the severe winter when my father brought me to London as he was conducting a couple of weddings. That visit impacted me in every way. I knew, at the age of eleven, that this was where I wanted to be in life. London was certainly battered, dark and grimy, with the remains of the crisscross tape still on many windows that was designed to prevent or at least reduce splintering glass panes during bombing raids. We stayed in the Celtic Hotel, close to Russell Square, owned by the London Welsh retired Mayor of St. Pancras. The food was quite sparse. I would leave my father on the hotel steps and head off to explore around Bloomsbury and Tottenham Court Road. My father did not chastise me for disappearing, however, he obviously felt he must take me somewhere and so I was marched off to the British Museum.

He placed me in front of some plaque and told me to translate the Latin text. I had already started learning some elementary Latin, helped by my brother John. My attempts at trying to translate faltered to a dead stop. I managed "sed" and "semper". It took me thirty years to return to the British Museum, but surely, I came to adore the venerable place.

During our fourteen years living in Bala, there was a particular household who were our special friends. This family consisted of our family doctor, Bob, and "Mrs Doctor Jones", as they would say in Wales, a lady named Nesta, their two daughters, Anne and Dilys, and Robert, who was a few years younger than me. Anne was a big friend of the twins and remained so all through their lives. As I grew into my later teens, I became particularly friendly with Dilys. My mother and Nesta were very involved with the little English Presbyterian church where my father would often preach. That would attract many who had, as it were, slipped away from any place of worship. The numbers would be augmented by numbers from Christ Church (Church of Wales). Even now, I can see Anne in a blue silk dress with a blue-ribboned boater of the same silk, and Dilys similarly dressed in pink. They looked so attractive with their stunningly rich red hair. We three children would be sitting behind, so it would be two families of all redheads.

Just a few years later, my father, who was not very happy with my schooling at the local grammar school, or else he did not want to accept that he had a dullard for a second son, sent me off to Monkton Combe outside Bath. This was a school founded for sons of the clergy. We hear of all kinds of tales against boarding schools, but Monkton was a modest one with a good academic grounding. The years I spent there were some happy ones, and I did become academically equipped, much to my father's relief, though I was not too pleased when my letters to home were corrected and marked with red ink for grammatical errors and then returned. Later on, I came to appreciate this. It was my father who took me all the way from Bala to Bath and my mother came to see me in the last term of all. Those of us whose parents never came at half term were perfectly happy and would go off to Bristol and thought we were ever so "with it". Imagine, we dared to go to La Ronde which, in the early fifties, was considered a rather risqué French film!

Whilst at boarding school, I was in the cadet force, known as the Corps, as it was the respectable thing to do and mandatory other than in name. I only knew of one boy who refused to be in the cadet force and so he was obliged to be in the Pioneer Corps. In the last term, four of us Upper Sixth boys were called for a medical examination in Bristol before some National Service medical committee. Three of us had already decided to present some medical history that might disqualify us from serving in the forces. However, one boy was set on entering the Army as his career. As things turned out, the three of us who thought we would escape serving were accepted at the third and lowest grade and the one who was intent on serving failed his medical on the grounds of eczema. When I was twelve or thirteen, I had had a TB scare and so had played on that to escape the army, but I was breezily told by the officer in charge of the medicals that what I needed was to be posted abroad to the Caribbean to have my lungs dried out. Instead of the Caribbean, I was posted to Scotland, England and Wales! My father took me to the station where I boarded the little local train from Bala and so ended those halcyon days of a Welsh boyhood.

PART 2

That arrival day at the Royal Artillery Garrison in Oswestry, the reception centre for the first two weeks, is well imprinted on my memory. Whilst these days my memory gets a little shaky, the impression of that day never does! And I am none the worse for that. It really was a hell on earth and a shock to one's system. Having been in the Cadet Force at school, I thought I was not some totally raw recruit and had some basic sense of discipline. It was all so fast-moving, starting with the first army haircut, or rather, complete head-shearing. About four of us sat in the barbers' chairs. I can see now the young man, around my age, with his Brylcreemed hair slicked back in the style that was fashionable at the time known as a DA - "duck's arse". He was wearing a purple knee-length coat with a black velvet collar. His shoes were known at that time as "brothel creepers", due to their very thick and soundless soles. He was absolutely mortified and watching him in the mirror, I could see he looked like he was in shock. I thought he was about to break into floods of tears.

Actually, I had no time to stop and see if he did weep as I was whisked into a room where I was issued with army kit and uniform and told to change immediately. A pair of boots, laces knotted together, were thrust around my neck and a second pair into my hands. Then we were marched to our barrack room. Still thinking I was something of an "old sweat", I rushed to the bed at the bottom end of the billet. There was a harsh shout from the other end: "Hey, Ginger! Get back right here. I want you close by me". He proved to be a real sadist who had taken an immediate dislike to me and how I spoke. For the rest of the two weeks, I seemed to be on non-stop fatigues like cleaning out kitchen cauldrons covered in grease, picking up papers on pathways or the parade ground and other demeaning tasks, even as early as dawn. Then it came to posting for actual basic training. I rushed to the posting sheets. I just wanted to get to the end of the world, as far away from this hell that was the Oswestry camp.

My destination was the Royal Artillery, Heavy AA (heavy guns) in Dundonald Camp in Troon, Ayrshire, set on the Firth of Clyde, which leads into the Atlantic, and right opposite the Isle of Arran with breathtaking sunsets. In contrast to Oswestry, in charge of us raw recruits was a tough Bombardier from the Black Country. He made it quite clear he was in charge and, if we did not give him trouble, he would look after us. Whilst in basic training, we were given bromide in our tea to check our libido and avoid erections! I know the bromide made the tea taste differently - very bitter unless you added what seemed like half a cupful of sugar. Bombardier wanted us to prove to be his best squad on the huge parade ground at the end of our basic training. We all ended up having great respect for him and were really sorry when we had to move on with no more of the Big Brother in our lives. He helped to shape many in the squad who otherwise would have ended up in and out of garrison jail, as did happen in the case of the purple-coated spiv with the once-DA hairdo. He was subsequently more often scalped or bristle-headed as he was in and out of the Regiment's jail (the glass house) regularly. After our passing out at the end of basic training, we ended up in beds next to each other. One night, with the wind off the Atlantic howling around the camp, we were cleaning our kit - mainly the brass buckles and uniform jewellery - the brooding spiv, looking into space, said, "I want to kill that Colonel of ours," a man whom we had, in fact, never really met, just glimpsed at the end of the parade ground. I jocularly replied, "That does not make me feel very safe in the bed next to you". He looked at me and said, "Oh, Ginger, I would never harm you; you are my mate and we're together in this situation!" However, I did meet the Colonel when I was summoned before him as he intended to refer me to OCTU (Officer Cadet Training Unit). However, I was simply not interested in becoming an officer. I just wanted to serve my time as an ordinary soldier, perhaps gaining a few stripes before I had completed my two years. The day came when I had to command a group of us soldiers on the parade ground. I was supposed to scream orders from the edge of the square and I knew my light voice would be lost in the distance. So, to my relief, that ended the Colonel's aspirations for me as a young officer of nineteen.

Now that we had "passed out" from basic training, it meant we were available for guard duty, which meant a parade before taking over from the daytime guard duty. We were dressed in overcoats and with shouldered rifles and a baton for self-defence when challenging a suspect in the dark of night. I remember one occasion, in the early hours in the pitch dark, patrolling amidst the sand dunes with the Isle of Arran across the water from us, and hearing a scuffle somewhere near a brick hut. I braced myself and shouted - probably sounding more like a squeak - "Stand forward and declare yourself! Produce your Identity Part 1 Passbook." By now, accustomed to the blackness, I had identified a human figure who seemed to be pressed against someone leaning on the brick wall. A voice quite coolly said, "It's okay, Ginger, it's only us". It was the Catering Corporal and Isabel from the NAAFI. My naivety was over. Some months later, I noticed that Isabel on NAAFI duty was somewhat swollen in the front. Following our meeting one another amidst the sand dunes, both the Corporal and Isabel were very generous - he at breakfast and she on my NAAFI visits.

Later, I was sent overnight with full kit to Woolwich, the Oxbridge of the Royal Artillery. Nowadays, it is all closed and many of the buildings have been converted into very elegant apartments and houses. The army food there was the best I ever had whilst serving my time. I had been sent for a typing course along with other convivial companions from across the UK. We were being trained to become clerks to serve back in the regiments we had come from. It was an easy time with no night guard duties, so we would rush up to Central London and dine at Scott's on the Strand and Lyon's Corner House where we would enjoy a carvery and a bottle of wine. Sometimes we would go to a Humphrey Lyttleton gig at the Dominion or some other venue. This life was too good and civilized to last.

About this time, my family moved all the way to Newcastle upon Tyne, Geordie Land and established our family home.

On my return to Troon, I settled into a general routine and, when off duty, would go to Ayr by the sea or Kilmarnock for "high tea" as they say in Scotland. Some months later, I was posted southward to Wales - so back to my roots. I was sent to the Royal Artillery Camp in Kinmel Park, a Garrison that also encompassed a Regiment of Royal Engineers, some of whom became friends, and we stayed in touch for some years. But of course, as time passes and one's life changes, many contacts fade away. Whilst at Kinmel, I became the Regimental Pay Clerk and earned two stripes to make me a Bombardier in the Royal Artillery - that is progress! During the last few months, some of us National Servicemen would be terminating our service every fortnight. As I was the Pay Clerk, I took on the responsibility for collecting the agreed weekly sum for the kitty to cover our fortnightly demob parties - the "piss-up" - when we knocked back pints of beer preceded by consuming a pint of milk and a fry-up to line the stomach with plenty of fat to cushion the beer. Later, however, most likely this would have been released on the colonel's rose beds, raising our berets to the colonel of the camp. In due course, it was my demob party. I do not recall any hangover from the party the following morning as I gleefully handed back my army kit.

Now a young man of 20, I was back in civilian clothes on Civvy Street on my way to join my parents and sister, who were now living in Newcastle upon Tyne, a city yet to be explored. I was out of the army too late to go to university in the new academic year, so, by the end of three weeks' demob leave, I was anxious to get some kind of job quickly, earn some money and recover my independence. After all, a cleric's son can hardly expect to live off his parents. So, I took myself to Bainbridge's, which had recently become part of the ever-expanding John Lewis Partnership. I thought it better not to mention that I was only looking for a temporary job; wisely so, as it proved to be. The Head of Personnel suggested that I go on the junior executive training scheme. And so, I was appointed to the Soft Furnishings department, firstly to net curtains - awful and so boring. Thank God it was not for long. This was in the infancy of plastics, even in furnishings. When a housewife asked for a quarter of a yard of sheet plastic for some kitchen shelf, I was so horrified that I almost biffed her on the head with the roll of sheet plastic I was about to cut. However, I was soon moved to actual soft furnishings with rolls of velvets, brocades and so on. On occasion, it became interesting when a very affluent couple came in having bought some castle up in the wilds of Northumbria that was needing a complete renovation. Then I had fun unwinding yards and yards of velvets and other fabrics. This seemed exciting and proved to be a big order. Still, most of the time it was dull.

The John Lewis Partnership has, or had in the past, many activities for its employees, especially the young. I immediately joined its very lively dramatic society and, in this way, my Welsh childhood interest in performing, whether in song or otherwise, returned instantly. It saved me. The society was thinking of next putting on a play called 'Trespass' by Emlyn Williams, a fellow countryman and special actor. I was already aware that the Geordies' speech has a particular lilt not that dissimilar to Welsh, particularly South Wales. Yet I felt confident that I could produce a real Welsh accent worthy of Wales, and, indeed, Emlyn Williams. And so, I got the part and revelled in the whole process, including the performances, in a little theatre across the Tyne in Gateshead. So, it was 'think no more of going to university but squeak not to your father'! I planned to make my life in the theatre. I said nothing to my parents. Instead, I arranged to talk to a good friend and admirer of my father's - William Drake, the boss of the YMC in Newcastle. He had many strings to his bow in the city and had already introduced my father to interesting connections both civically and academically. I knew that Drake had a connection with the Director of the Playhouse Theatre in Newcastle which was quite close to my home. Of course, the Playhouse operated on a shoestring, so I was engaged as an Assistant Stage Manager (ASM) at £3 a week and told I was lucky to get that. I told Bainbridge's forthwith that I would be leaving at the end of the week, and it was not till then that I told my parents. It was such a bombshell to my father that he was speechless! But I saw my mother with such a smile on her face. I could tell it had revived her own interest in going to Birmingham's music halls and later to theatres, to which she took me during and post-wartime, and this had sown the earliest seeds of my own interest.

As I write, I recall my arrival at the Playhouse pass door directly from the road and up a few steps onto the side of the stage, there to come face to face with the young Judith Gibson, Judy Gobbo, the ASM straight out of RADA, the Royal Academy of Dramatic Art, and proud of her elocuted voice. She was sweeping the stage and said, "Here you are, here's the brush. I've been doing this for too long." The whole place was infused with the musky smell of size and greasepaint, not just backstage but also around the front of house. That in itself added to the excitement. This was a Monday, a very long day and the dress rehearsal leading into the first night of a new production. The working schedule for the week was based on the play being performed every night, another being rehearsed for the next week and a third play being read and learnt by the actors for the third week. On the Monday, there was never time for the stage management, now three of us, to have any breaks. My dear mother had sent me off to this first day of a life in real theatre with my packed victuals of beautiful sandwiches, fruit, crisps and chocolate for energy. Her sandwiches were always a joy to all the family, especially for journeys, and now, for me in weekly rep. The first play was 'To Dorothy A Son' by Roger MacDougall and the actor who played the husband was called David K Grant. He had large brown eyes that worked overtime. He was very funny and beautifully "camp", a word still strong in the theatre describing many things, not just one's sexuality. Well, that was so in those days. We used the French word "Alors" often - pronouncing the "s" at the end of the word, which made it quite un-French - as an exclamation and meaning something outrageous. Because the turnover of actors and stage management was frequent, I was elevated to Stage Manager within a matter of weeks.

A new Director of Productions, John Ingram, who I met once later in my early years in London, was a source of great encouragement and inspiration for me in those formative days. We worked well together. He taught me how to select music for several of his productions. It was he who introduced me to Vaughan Williams' 'Fantasia on a Theme' by Thomas Tallis which has remained with me ever since. I like to listen to it in total silence and stillness. John secured plays quickly after release from the West End for release around the repertory theatre circuit in the provinces/regions. Sadly, he did not stay too long in repertory theatre on a pittance salary and far from London. He was succeeded by someone from New Zealand who had an awful grating voice and would cast himself in parts that were quite unsuitable for his harsh voice and personality. The company was changing ever more frequently. So, with two years in weekly rep, I decided to get out and make for the unknown in London. (I suppose the one sure theme in my life is moving ever into the "unknown" as it would prove to be.)

My brother John, who was working in London at the time, lived in Belsize Park in a somewhat dilapidated and poorly furnished flat shared with two flatmates and their accompanying and often-changing women. Being landed with the kid brother on the premises was not exactly what John's flatmates wanted around the place. As it was, the large bed allocated to me had to be vacated by 8 am in time for the Viennese girlfriend of one of the flatmates, a nurse, returning from night duty. Well, I was also not particularly happy with the arrangement. Fortunately, Margaret, my future sister-in-law and good friend through the rest of her life, was very anxious to get John out of the flat to a bedsit before their wedding in a matter of months. Margaret found him a dowdy bedsit with a single gas ring. I think tins of Heinz baked beans and sausage were his staple diet. Fortunately, Margaret had qualified in domestic science, so John landed on all four paws for the rest of his life as Margaret was a great cook.

Cousins of my father took pity on me, and Olwen, the cousin's wife, found me a place in Kilburn, right opposite the tube station, known as the Gentlemen's Guest House. I became quickly accustomed to the constant rattling of the tube trains and the bridge over the Guest House, which catered for young men from Wales working or studying in London. The place was run by two London/Welsh sisters in their 60s, Bessie and Lina. Bessie had a rather mottled face with red hair that was bottled up every few months on the sisters' regular visits to Selfridges to top up the bed linen and general housekeeping supplies. She was rather a bundle of nerves and agitated by her large and sedentary sister Lina, who similarly bottled her hair at Selfridges but in blue. She was a chain smoker, as was the custom in those days. Likewise, Lina's husband Griff smoked heavily. However, the food was really good, with wholesome meals provided by Bessie on a large dining table in the basement. Every three months (only), the sisters would go to the Welsh Presbyterian Church in Willesden Green and magnanimously provide the flowers for the Sunday. The only reason they went to Chapel every three months was to ensure that they would not be excommunicated for lack of attendance. One Monday evening, we young men were deep into our "hay bags" around the table enjoying supper when this particular lodger from Cardiff asked Lina, smoking by the fireside as usual, "Where did you get these beautiful gladiolis from?" (This was before we had met Edna Everage and her "gladis"). Lina retorted, "From the Chapel of course. We were not going to leave them there to die!"

Having a bath had to be booked in advance. It could be quite precarious, as I remember one occasion when a train rattled overhead and down came a torrent of metal shavings from the water tank overhead, leaving me looking as if I'd been covered in potato peelings. Among us young Taffy gentlemen was a young student,

Martin, who attended St. Martin's Art College and who often liked to sleep off yet another late night. Bessie and Lina aimed to have breakfast over by 9 am. Often, Bessie would rush up from the basement shouting, "Martin, get up!" She would bang on his door and barge into his room and pull away his bedclothes. She did so one morning and there he was, lying in supposed slumber, in a state of total nudity. Bessie screamed with horror and rushed downstairs; an incident that appeared straight from Dylan Thomas's 'Under Milkwood'! Soon afterwards, along with one of my inmates from Shoot-up Hill, I moved to newly converted bedsits in a one-time "villa" with a kitchenette, a washbasin and two divans. I seem to remember one bathroom on the first floor for the whole house. Fridges were not available for general usage in those days.

As soon as I arrived in London, I had to find some work as my meagre savings would not last that long. I found a boring but useful job for my immediate purposes at the London County Council (LCC), County Hall, South Bank, later elevated to the Greater London Council until Margaret Thatcher hammered it out of existence. I was employed as a temporary filing clerk which was ever so boring. However, it covered my moderate living expenses. My supper would frequently be spaghetti Bolognese and a pint of Keg Bitter at the first Spaghetti House in London on Goodge Street. As a treat to myself, I would go to the famous Schmidt's on Charlotte Street, complete with its sanded floor, and have what seemed at the time a heavenly Wiener Schnitzel, etc.

Whilst at County Hall, I found two kindred spirits, both from Ireland, Anne Keily from the Southwest and Tommy from Tralee. Anne was a beautifully wild and devout Catholic and introduced me to London Irish friends and to Irish Whiskey, and that remains a great spiritual interest to me. She had escaped from Ireland as a nursing postulant who was asked to leave by the Superior. She used to say, "I'll have you on your knees before the Holy Father," and I would respond, "Never, never!". I found my own way there a little later just in time before Pope John XIII died and after Anne Keily had returned to the Emerald Isle.

The boring work at County Hall enabled me at lunchtime to rush across Hungerford Bridge alongside the constant trains rushing across to and from Charing Cross Station and Waterloo. I would dash up to various theatre agents in the West End hoping to find stage management vacancies in various pending productions. I would queue up for listing on any advert jobs. Then, at 4.30, I would rush across the bridge again to apply for various showmen jobs in the West End shows whether as a stagehand, or on electrics/lighting, or as an extra propman. Many people would work in the evenings as a dresser but that never came my way. As I was finding my own way, I really only had one thing in mind, namely, to have a good foundation In what we innocents termed "Classical Theatre". I was all set to get a start in the Old Vic. So, almost every week, I would plague the Stage/ Technical Director about any vacancies in stage management. He was so patient and never suggested I should try in six months' time if only to get me off his back. Later, I discovered that Bill Bundy at the Royal Opera House had contacted the Old Vic Technical Director, who I was plaguing weekly, as he might have some suggestions of possible ASM positions from the Director of the Vic, Glen Byam Shaw, a great friend of Robert Helpmann, an ex-Principal Dancer of the Royal Ballet who partnered Margot Fonteyn. As in other areas of working life, often, through connections and otherwise, things can happen that you don't expect!

Part 3

One day, shortly before 4.30 pm, as I was about to leave County Hall for my evening job in some West End theatre, the telephone rang and it was for me. Never before in my time at County Hall had the phone rung for me. That call changed my London life – well, really my whole life. It was a call from the Royal Opera House, Covent Garden. Lyn Siddons, secretary for the Stage/Technical Director, the fierce Bill Bundy, wanted to arrange an interview for the position of Assistant Stage Manager for the Royal Ballet. As I had never approached the Royal Opera House regarding any work vacancies, either in opera or ballet, I was quite perplexed. Of course, I was excited, but nonetheless, somewhat confused. Lyn said that she would get back to me next day with a date. I virtually swam across the Thames to my evening showman's job in the West End. These days, I cannot quite remember the theatre, though I think it might have been the Garrick. The next day came and I was poised for my call but it did not come. It was the same with the following two days.

Despite the adage "Hope springs Eternal", bitterness sank in as I said to myself, "Here we go again; so many hopes but all seem to die quick enough". Finally, however, the call came with the date. This was early 1960. I donned my one and only suit as we did in those days and arrived in Covent Garden market with the porters wheeling their loads of vegetables over already crushed and smashed vegetables, cursing and swearing with every four-letter word. Ringing from above was the voice of a soprano rehearsing in some studios in 45 Floral Street, opposite the stage door. Once immersed in Covent Garden, I came to recognise the voice that duetted with the effing and blinding from the porters as belonging to Amy Shuard in Aida. Many years later, her studio became part of the Royal Ballet School. I just loved this real mix of divine music and the profanity and reality of the market industry.

Lyn met me at the stage door and took me up in the brass cage lift to Bill Bundy's office. On first meeting him, he was almost gentle compared to how he was after a few years. There was, as I had experienced at the Playhouse Theatre in Newcastle upon Tyne, the similar pervading smell of size and scenic paint that permeated everywhere backstage. This is something I still miss in my life today - the warmth and cosiness. The job as ASM would have to be ratified by Dame Ninette de Valois, Director and Founder of The Royal Ballet, who ruled with a rod of iron and who was always known and addressed as Madam. Bill said his secretary would confirm the date for me to see Madam - "La Generalissima". So again, I sailed out of the stage door into an amalgam of expletives, crushed vegetables, fruit and arias. Then there was the waiting for that telephone to ring again. Perhaps I was a little chastened and hardened to waiting, but the call did come. So, the same one suit was donned. This time, another secretary, Joanne Dixon, Madam's secretary, collected me at the stage door and took me up in the brass cage lift to the paint frame level, then to the other side of the stage and down a flight of really solid stone steps. We went through the very small and pokey switchboard, more like a cupboard manned by the boss, Betty Evans, who gave me the once-over, then into another pokey cupboard, the office of the secretary to the General Manager, which led into the man himself, Michael Wood. He was very tall and elegant and had a very particular rather high-pitched voice, especially for his height. He gestured for me to sit more beside his desk as James, his tiny Jack Russell, could not be disturbed from his cushioned chair opposite Michael. To add to the mix of life on, in and off Floral Street, it was somehow reassuring to see Michael walking serenely with James, his four-legged friend in tow - the long and the short of it... Michael spoke kindly, perhaps preparing me before entry to the inner sanctum. Bill had told me that Madam had just returned from a wedding and may have enjoyed champagne which could help things. Her office was certainly bigger than the cupboards leading to her, but not so much. She was dressed in a silk suit, suitable for a wedding, with a stole around her, the tails of which she had thrown around her neck. I was told to sit at the other side of the desk. I noticed she had a yellow aide memoire on her blotting pad which she would peer at occasionally and I realized it contained some basic details about me.

She suddenly said, "I see you play the piano." Startled, and not knowing what might be expected of ballet stage management, I replied, "I learnt to play as a child but I do not play really these days". "That does not matter but at least you have an understanding and appreciation of music and that is essential when working with the ballet. I see you have been working in repertory theatre. I have no time for the West End." Thank God I had not mentioned that most evenings I worked as a showman in the West End! "And now," she said, "you will join the Company as soon as possible and will learn the current repertoire. Later, in August, you will go with the Company to the Edinburgh Festival with a completely different repertoire. Afterwards, the Company will go to America for a six-month tour starting with a six-week season at the Metropolitan Opera House in New York. After that, the Company will tour coast to coast including Canada. I want to tell you something; you will learn more about everything in life in that time than you ever will at the Opera House in two years!" And she was dead right. Everything she said was emphatically stated. I realized she was The Commander.

For about three years after that, she never seemed to know who I was. I managed to leave the boring LCC job at the end of the week and so started on the Monday at the Royal Opera House, again crushing dropped vegetables on the way through Covent Garden with an amalgam of profanities of the time from the market porters interspersed with some opera singer practising in No. 45 opposite the stage door. So, my life really started there. The Deputy Stage Manager, Leon Arnold, met me at the stage door and led me along a dank under-stage corridor to the canteen for coffee. That corridor was to become so much a constant in my life for many years. Yes, coffee with some of the first-year corps de ballet girls. I instantly felt welcomed into this friendly atmosphere, both within the ballet company, and indeed, with whoever else I met whether from the Opera, technical, or front-of-house staff.

Initially, everything seemed to move very fast. I had arrived very soon after the triumph of Frederick Ashton's wonderful and bucolic 'La Fille Mal Gardée' with the fabulous cast of Nadia Nerina, David Blair, Alexander Grant, Stanley Holden and Leslie Edwards. This was quickly followed by Kenneth McMillan's one -act ballet 'Le Baiser de la Fée', with the beautiful

Svetlana Beriosova, like a burning piece of ice, cold caustic soda, with darting Slavic eyes, Lynn Seymour and Donald MacLeary with Kenneth Rowell's very fine designs. Those early days were intoxicating and were the seeds of my growing love for ballet/dance, and indeed, for dancers. These days, I do not go to the ballet so much but certainly, I have mostly happy and indelible memories which linger with me in retirement in Wapping.

The day finally came when I was to stage-manage a Saturday matinee of 'Le Lac des Cygnes' (Swan Lake) as it was titled in print in those days and always called Lac in the Company by both staff and dancers. I was told quite definitely that if I could not manage then I would have to leave. I went away with the prompt score to study alongside a recording of the music. Firstly, the prompt (piano) score was a complete mess with cue changes rubbed and scratched out. The music sounded and seemed quite different to what was in the prompt score. So, come the Saturday, I was so nervous and thought I would be kicked out of the stage door after the performance, or certainly by the end of the next week. As I was expected to make the various calls to the dancers and staff for the performance, I checked into the prompt corner way before the first half-hour call to try to make sense of the music. However, dear Bill McGee, the chief electrician, arrived in the corner nonchalantly. I suppose he saw me looking anxious and he tapped me on the shoulder and said, "Just you give me the cues where you think they go, and I will do the same where I think they go, and we will get there together." I will never forget him for that and I hope the harps are serenading him up in the clouds. We later discovered that by birth, we were both Scousers.

That production, with Leslie Hurry's stage designs and Tania Moiseiwitsch's costume designs, was the easiest to stage-manage, and very quickly, I learnt it by heart without needing that dreadful prompt copy. Later, when I was a senior in the job, I made new prompt/production scores similar to those in opera and general theatre. Some years later, I used to do the same for Madam after her retirement from the company - not that she ever really retired - when she would be off on her sorties, usually to mount Lac and her brilliantly conceived and executed 'The Rake's Progress' in Turkey. That ballet is an excellent and inspired piece of true dance/theatre.

Soon after the 'Swan Lake' Saturday matinee, I was sent to experience the ballet from up in the dome of the opera house in which there was a real artist operating - John Knight. He would travel daily from Brighton to London. The dome was his domain from where he follow-spotted leading artists in ballet and opera, and then, after a long or short performance, he travelled back home to Brighton. He was a quiet man and such a sensitive operator and artist at work.

By this time, we had come to the end of the season which would have been midsummer. The last performance, on the eve of the annual summer holiday, was 'Le Lac des Cygnes' with Svetlana Beriosova as Odette/Odile and Donald MacLeary as her Prince Siegfried. It was also the last performance of Julia Farron, who was retiring as a full member of the Company, though she was a permanent guest artist for many years. On this last night, she was partnered by Alexander Grant. That was the most electrifying performance of the Neapolitan pas de deux I have ever seen in my life, and I have seen many! Both Julia and Alexander were very special artists/dancers.

So, the Company went off on the summer break while I went to Barcelona and to the little fishing village of Sitges on the Mediterranean. It was a very modest place where sardines were cooked on the beach and local women came with embroidery to sell to sunbathers. It was quite a different place to what it developed into soon afterwards, a gay's paradise, before the word had changed its meaning. Well, not really, for its meaning of "joy" has lasted. The marvels of the English language!

After the holidays, we were back to rehearsals to prepare for crossing the Border to the Edinburgh Festival in the Athens of the North. This is a place so full of history that in our own time, it may well define our history ever more firmly; a force that England will have to reckon with. This will give Wales encouragement and perhaps will calmly lead to the union of Ireland that can harmonise the whole of Britannia. The repertoire for the week in Edinburgh was: Baiser, La Péri, Danses Concertantes, Ballabile, Firebird and one other which I cannot remember.

We returned to London to almost immediately fly off to New York for a six-week season at the old Metropolitan Opera House that was soon to be totally demolished. It had the most beautiful gold curtain which was sold off in squares at a dollar a piece. The biennial tours of the Royal Ballet to New York and around the United States and Canada were renowned for the prestige and fame the Company brought and the income it attracted for the Royal Opera House. Yes, I remember quite vividly the starriness of the season. In my lowly position, I spent all performances amidst the heat of the spot bar above and behind the proscenium arch from where I cued the two New York operators to follow-spot the leading dancers. 'Sleeping Beauty', with the famous Oliver Messel designs, opened the season, led by the Goddess of the Dance - Margot Fonteyn – as Princess Aurora, nobly partnered by Michael Somes - Prince Florimund, Alexander Grant - Carabosse, and Leslie Edwards, such an elegant Catalabutte - being master of the Court of Louis Quatorze. Annette Page and Brian Shaw were unforgettable as the dazzling Bluebirds. For the Lilac Fairy, the very young and so graceful Deanna Bergsma had emerged. This must have launched her on a fine career with such distinguished roles to follow, not least as The Hostess in 'Les Biches' (The Does) after Svetlana Beriosova. The young Merle Park, Maryon Lane and Donald MacLeary sparkled as Florestan and his sisters, across and around the stage. After the opening night, the impresario, the inimitable Sol Hurok, gave a party for the whole company. What I remember from that was Margot Fonteyn in a fabulous golden shimmering dress dancing with a rather drunken Sviatoslav Richter and they stopped the dance floor with their antics.

The rest of the six-week season was full of repertoire treats for somebody new to the riches within ballet. Not least for me was John Cranko's 'Antigone' - a piece of ballet theatre with most unusual stage and costume designs. Sadly, I think the ballet did not survive the American tour. Of course, Sir Frederick Ashton's ballets were always a success in New York and this season, 'La Fille Mal Gardée' and 'Ondine' were equally so. Apart from Fonteyn's creation of the water spirit Ondine, Lila di Nobili's stage sets and costumes were so beautiful and evocative and lit so effectively by Michael Northen.

After performances, many of us would pile into Bill's Bar opposite the stage door and order our Bill or John Collins, a concoction of whisky or gin on the rocks. I would often make my way home to our hotel via other bars where I was guaranteed some wonderful Black jazz bands and nips of Scotch.

After the six weeks at the old Metropolitan Opera House in Times Square, we set off on the rest of the six-month tour of the USA and Canada from Grand Central Station on the special Royal Ballet train. And it really was a special train, just like the one in "Some like It Hot" - that real classic from the past with Marilyn Monroe, Tony Curtis and Jack Lemmon - never to be forgotten.

Our first stop on the tour was East Lansing and the first student campus I had experienced at the time. Although I now cannot remember the exact order of the places we visited, there were twenty-nine cities and towns altogether, including Canada, where we visited Vancouver, Montreal and Toronto.

We were now somewhere in the Mid-West which already seemed endless. The Company were well settled in the Royal Ballet train, and into continental touring, it seemed. On the other side of the train corridor from me, the happy quartet of Svetlana Beriosova, Georgina Parkinson, Donald MacLeary and Graham Usher was playing cards and shrieking with laughter, supported by their dixie cups. There was a sudden cry of alert that we had hit a dry state, so the cups were quickly hidden. This was done with alacrity by these professionals! The train came to a stop and we all piled off and onto the rail track. Our special train crew alerted us to re-embark and soon we were chuntering off westwards. To me, the novice, everything was new and exciting. Of course, we were young and some of us were in the New World for the very first time, so we naturally bonded together. Some had already formed relationships in New York. Removed from the grandeur of the Royal Opera House, Covent Garden, and indeed, of the glamour of the old Metropolitan Opera House, New York, we had already become the gypsies in our special caravan - the Royal Ballet Train that had also become Some Like It Hot in many ways!

Soon after the Midwest, we arrived in Sacramento. What I remember of the place was when looking for somewhere to eat in the evening, there were three small shops next door to each other with vivid advertising lighting. There was a funeral shop displaying coffins which were lit up with 'HOUSE FOR OUR LOVED ONES' and then a florist with a sign saying, 'SAY IT WITH FLOWERS' and finally a butcher's saying, 'TENDER MEAT'! From there, we may have gone direct to The Shrine, Los Angeles, later replaced by an Opera House. After a while, the company had a few days free. So, Leon Arnold, the Deputy Stage Manager, rented a Chevrolet for six of us - himself, Pamela Moncur, Deanne Bergsma, Keith Rosson, Luanne Richards and me - to drive further south into Mexico. At Tijuana, the frontier check point, five of us passed through without a hitch. But poor Deanne was detained in a grubby cell because of her South African passport. So, Leon and I stayed with Deanne whilst he tried to resolve the issue which took some wrangling. After this, we found somewhere to eat some rather miserable food then went to an even more miserable and hideous lesbian show. We had booked into a motel - my first experience of this. The following morning early, we drove off southwards towards Ensenada in our newly acquired Chevrolet alongside the silent and deserted Pacific. We spent the day lying on the empty sands or in and out of the Pacific's healing waters with the girls draped in seaweed. Much later, I paid the price with my lily-white Celtic/Welsh skin. All too soon we had to leave our paradise. My back was already stinging and looking like a tomato. The 'kids' placed me in the motel shower and one of them suggested pouring milk onto my back - it sucked it up like blotting paper. However, we managed to have a good dinner with a couple of Margaritas - my first - in Ensenada. Next morning, we drove northwards bound for San Diego where we were performing two nights before rushing back to complete the Los Angeles season.

We were already into November and would then be travelling, RB-style, to San Francisco for a two-week season at the Opera House. This was when JF Kennedy won the US Presidency. I fell in love with San Francisco and the sight of the Golden Gate Bridge despite the constant cloud and drop in temperature. Whilst all the "guns" were brought out for this amazing city, one of the performances that remains with me to this day is that of (Dame) Merle Park as Lise in 'La Fille Mal Gardée'. Backstage, things were becoming rather fractious between the American and British technical crews. In one performance, one of the US electrics had rigged up a mock prop for checking so-called electrics and would apply it in the dark of backstage during performances, as he did to me. He pressed the battery and kept it pressed against my posterior. I remember seeming to soar up a height. The Americans thought it a great laugh, but I felt the stinging until the next day. Meanwhile, our Prop Master, Alfie, had seen this happening. The next night was a 'Sleeping Beauty' performance and in Act Three (The Awakening Scene), there is a big scene change so our Prop Master was checking and he knew that the American culprit would be close at hand. Alfie returned the compliment given to me the night before which sent the American flying off the stage yelling, fortunately, masked by the Tchaikovsky coming from the orchestra pit.

Before we left San Francisco, it was Christine Antony's 21st birthday and so a few of us decided to take her for a birthday dinner in the famous Top of the Mark overlooking San Francisco Bay and to the Ella Fitzgerald concert in Top of the Mark. Whilst we were sitting with our pre-dinner drinks, we realised that sitting all alone and very close by was Nat King Cole. Christine nearly swooned on seeing him. So, I said, "Shall I ask him for his autograph on your menu?"

I explained that it was her special birthday. He smiled, saying, "Bring the young lady over, please," indicating the one seat opposite him. He raised his hand, calling with his velvety voice, "Champagne for the lady, please," with such charm. After our dinner, we went to the fabulous Ella concert in which there was a heckler; probably a drunk. Ella had a white chiffon scarf that she kept stroking whilst she sang mesmerically until he crept away. Unsurprisingly, we and the audience gave her an ovation, and again at the end too. Such an artist.

All too soon, we were off to Portland where the Fall colours were spectacular, then off to Vancouver in a different country. Perhaps the best sensation was having a real cup of tea like home where the kettle water was boiled to completion. I had become used to my hot rod tea bought in some US drug store where the water does not completely boil. In those days, one was not aware of the Chinese population and skyscrapers in the city. I was more aware of shortbread and women in Fair Isle jumpers and tweed skirts because the Chinese hordes had not arrived at that time but the Scottish influence was apparent. All these many years later, I am sure it is no longer obvious. From Vancouver, we must have flown to Montreal. There was no Opera House or theatre large enough to take the Ballet, so the company performed on an ice rink on a specially built stage. It was already really cold. From there, we must have gone to Toronto, to the newly built O'Keefe Centre, to be later renamed the Meridian Hall. We opened with Margot Fonteyn and Michael Somes in 'Giselle'. As the theatre was brand new, it had all the latest stage equipment at the time. This included the elevating and lowering of the orchestra pit. So, Music Director, John Lanchbery was instructed to press his red button when ready and the pit would rise to the level already set and tested. However, instead, the pit rose and rose above the level of the stage and continued upwards. The auditorium was a house of roaring laughter and Jack turned to them and bowed and roared too. Backstage there was panic. Fonteyn, being the absoluta of artists, just cooly waited and so did the audience. After the performance, I was able to meet my Welsh cousin and his Canadian wife Betty who took us for dinner and back to their charming home where, for the first time, I met little Miss Janet, one of three, who I have seen often over the years. I could see that Betty would fairly soon be increasing the family with John and, sometime later, Laura. In my old age, I enjoy our strong trans-Atlantic alliance. We have maintained a purely Celtic connection of Scottish, Irish and Welsh (me).

We travelled by train to New Orleans for I remember the vast waterway and immense viaduct/bridgeway into the city. What was something of a shock was the segregation of blacks and whites. (I use the terminology of the time.) Blacks had to sit at the back of buses. There were separate drinking taps for black people and likewise, the toilets were also segregated. That really was horrifying. Otherwise, the city seemed one of the prettiest in the USA. And the food was some of the best in the USA on the tour to date. From there, we must have travelled by our "Some Like it Hot" train to Birmingham, Alabama, where it was snowing. The Black people (Black Americans, please, David) looked so sad and cold in the snow. From there we went by train overnight to Washington, DC. Suddenly, in the night, there was a huge bang as we had hit a large tree which had fallen across the rail track during the heavy blizzards. What I remember most about Washington was the sparkling snow and brilliantly blue skies, the White House, which is beautifully white, and governmental buildings and wide-open main avenues and streets strangely reminiscent of past European imperial cities - Vienna, St Petersburg (Leningrad), Berlin and Madrid. It was a complete joy to visit Washington National Gallery with its glorious contents. And I remember the sight of Monica Mason, future Director of the Royal Ballet and Dame, at that time in her mock red fur coat. The red of her coat seemed ablaze in the midst of the crisp snow all around.

We then flew from Washington to Boston where we performed on an ice rink for a couple of performances, and yes, it was really cold despite the heating provided on stage and for the backstage accommodation. Then we must have flown to Chicago for a two-week season at the Opera House. Chicago seemed really exciting despite the cruel winds that blew off Lake Michigan and round the blocks to and from the hotel and Opera House. It was a Chicago Christmas and great fun sharing Christmas gifts. A few of us, mostly from the Corps de ballet and me, managed to go to Midnight Mass. The premier dancer, Michael Somes, gave me a slim tie and thanked me for being so calm in my stage management which I took as a compliment since I had avoided some of his outbursts of rage.

We were still in Chicago for New Year. Gerd Larsen was one of the senior members of the company and married to Harold Turner, Director of the Opera Ballet at the Opera House in London. He had been one of the Principal Dancers of the Company who had created the role of the Red Knight in Dame Ninette's ballet 'Checkmate' that she had created at the end of the 1930s. Gerd and Harold wanted to go and celebrate New Year with Company friends so she asked me if I would babysit. I was delighted to help. They both told me to help myself to whatever I fancied out of the fridge which was full of goodies and booze. Little Solveig was an absolute angel - I did not empty the fridge but did enjoy some of the contents.

From Chicago, I think we went on to Baltimore for a couple of performances and finally to Rochester where I caught some stomach bug and had to see the American Company doctor. He gave me a jab, or shot as Americans say, in the posterior and the bug vanished by the next day. Mind you, there is a theatre saying - "Doctor Theatre" will get you through - i.e., "the show must go on." On one of the days in Rochester, a few of us, Leon Arnold, Jack Hart, Anne Howard, his wife then, Pamela Moncur and I went to Niagara Falls which is quite close to Rochester. The American side of the Falls is smaller than the Canadian side, which is quite terrifying. I experienced that about ten years ago when visiting my Canadian cousins in Ontario.

Then, at last - and we were all ready to return home - we travelled to New York for some TV film (I think) with Fonteyn and Somes. I think it was only a couple of days' work at most. At last, the joy of arriving back in London. At Heathrow, the whole Company quickly dispersed across to their various London homes. After a short break, just a few days, the Company returned to Barons Court and to their daily routine and the staff and stage management went back to Covent Garden amidst the ever-busy marketeers with their barrows and crushed vegetables. In residence were the Royal Ballet Touring Company, who had covered for the Resident Company over Christmas, including two world premieres – in November, Kenneth McMillan's very daring (for the time) 'The Invitation', which included a rape scene. The other two ballets were Andrée Howard's revival of 'Veneziana', and 'Les Deux Pigeons' (title changed to Two Pigeons and less evocative), which premiered at the Opera House in February with the stunning young Christopher Gable as the young artist, Lynn Seymour as his love and the seductive and menacing Elizabeth Anderton as the gypsy lover who seduces the young artist. And... there were two live pigeons! As there were only three ballet performances at the Garden, I was drafted to the Touring Company to help with the stage management, little thinking it would change the course of my life with Royal Ballet before the end of the year. The Touring Company were soon back to touring the Regions before setting off on a tour in South Africa and Rhodesia, as it was then known. The London season at Covent Garden finished on a Saturday night in early June with 'Le Lac des Cygnes', as it was still called, with Svetlana Beriosova and Donald MacLeary in the title roles.

In those days, there were ballet fans who were able to sit in the cheapest seas in the "Gods" - the Upper/Upper Circle. There was sadness when they disappeared a few years later due to ever-increasing ticket prices and rearranging of seating and pricing to gain maximum returns, even from the gods!

Meanwhile, we carried on at the Garden with the rest of the London season before going off to Russia - Leningrad and Moscow. This was a postponed visit as the Company had been due to go in 1956 but the trip had to be cancelled because of the Hungarian Revolution. Of course, this was something very special as Russia was considered the cradle of classical ballet. We set off as the advance party consisting of three stage management and the stage/technical staff on 7 June 1961. At that time, (and so it is again in Summer 2022!) the Soviet Union was a firmly closed world. Our small gang, the vanguard, went to prepare the staging for when the dancers and other staff arrived for the stage rehearsals prior to the opening performance. I know we left London by BOAC to Moscow then were in transit on a flight with Aeroflot from Moscow to Leningrad (St. Peterburg). We were met by a welcoming party and driven directly to the historic Astoria Hotel, then looking shabby but nonetheless reminiscent of the Chekhovian age with chenille curtains and tablecloths. On each floor, there were "Babooshki" in command of all the door keys.

The repertoire for the Russian tour was 'La Fille Mal Gardée', 'Ondine', 'Sleeping Beauty'; then two triple bills (not in the correct order) – 'Les Patineurs', 'Lady and the Fool', 'Firebird', 'Danses Concertantes', 'Rinaldo and Armida' and 'Rake's Progress'.

The next morning, we, the advance party, reported to the Kirov Opera House and the home of the Kirov Ballet, formerly the Mariinsky Ballet and Opera house. It was then, and is still for me, the most beautiful opera house of all that I know. It is all soft blues of silk, paint and cream and gold plaster and carpeting. Following the destruction and siege of the Nazis in World War 2, and with the collapse of the Soviet regime in 1991, it has been refurbished and restored to its pre-Revolution times.

All the staff we dealt with could not have been more helpful. And we were blessed with Alla, our chief interpreter, who was truly professional and true to every word translated. Her own authorities could never accuse her of skating the parameters of her job. She was indeed somewhat aristocratic in behaviour and features with such deep blue eyes and a classical nose. She made me think of a younger Princess Marina, our Duchess of Kent at the time. Each day, when we finished preparing the stage, we would insist on walking her home along the great River Neva, but we would come to a point when she would raise her hand and say, "Please, no further. Spasibo, (thank you) no further." The rest of the Company arrived in a few days and so did a number of other interpreters to help the dancers, ballet and music staff and of course, the wardrobe which was quite colossal. On stage, it was interesting to see the number of females within the stage and properties staff. I can see vividly now one older gentle-faced woman, along with her male comrades, rolling a stage cloth. Out of her cleavage slipped an Orthodox cross. She caught my eye and, looking left and right, covered it and returned it to her bosom.

We opened the season with 'La Fille Mal Gardée' with the original cast that had a triumph in London the previous year - Nadia Nerina, David Blair, Stanley Holden, Alexander Grant and Leslie Edwards. As in London, this opening ballet in Leningrad was a total triumph. The audiences for all performances were so warm and encouraging. One could feel their knowledge about ballet. And I think we also felt we were in the cradle of classical ballet.

During this season, I would walk from the Astoria Hotel, to the Kirov Opera House, crossing over the Moika Canal that would get me to the artists' entrance of the Kirov, now restored to the original pre-Revolution name of Mariinsky Opera House. Suddenly, I heard running behind me. The young man caught up, walking beside me saying, "You are English, or French or American. I give you good exchange." I said, "I have no money. We are just poor artists." He kept walking with me until we reached the Opera House on the corner and then he dashed away.

I cannot remember if we presented both triple bill programmes but 'Sleeping Beauty' was reserved strictly for Moscow as the last programme of all.

Being in Leningrad in mid-June, we were there at the time of the White Nights. The night of another 'La Fille Mal Gardée' meant we finished very early for theatre folk, already having had our evening meal, though it could take over an hour to be served. We must have been at least 90 strong. So, because of the White Nights, some of us -corps de ballet, me and a few others

- decided to go on one of the holiday boats on the Neva. There was a rickety gramophone playing some dance music. There were some Leningrad University students also on board and quickly there were exchanges with the dancers. Before leaving London, we had been given a pep talk at the British Council on what we could and should not do, such as photographing queues for food and currency exchange, etc. Most of us had taken pictures of our young Queen Elizabeth, Westminster Abbey, the Houses of Parliament, Buckingham Palace, etc. Soon, the dance music changed to the conga. So, we all linked up to conga around the boat. Everything seemed blissfully innocent and refreshing, seeing these young people having a great time. But that is not how the authorities saw things. Then another evening with an early finish and a long wait over dinner, the company decided to make their own party. We were all seated at individual tables which seemed amassed with international flags. I think we took the cue from one of the Principals' tables who just cleared it of flags and bottles and so a cabaret started. Our dear General Manager, Michael Wood, took the floor partnered by Stanley Holden - the long and short of it all. Stanley would lift Michael, who lifted his long arms to heaven whooping, and with that, one of the other interpreters, Lilla, so beautifully camp, leapt across the floor with a pink peony between her teeth to place beneath Michael's long, long legs shouting, "I am in love with Michael!"

I think that was the denouement of our cabaret and the last we saw of dear Lilla.

The next day, Madam called us all into her suite. She had been told by the Civic Authorities - the KGB no doubt - that the Company had caused hooliganism the night of the Neva boat happiness, and also of our hotel cabaret and the removal of flags from tables. All I can remember her saying was that we must be careful how we behaved and that we were in Russia as ambassadors for our country - or words to that effect. She then went on to say that she had received great praise from the Russian ballet aficionados for the high standard of technique and particularly the footwork and musicality. However, she then said, "So, I asked Sergei, the Director, what he would say is our weakest and he said the backs." Now, it is not I who should pass on this detail as I'm not an authority on ballet technique but since I remember the quote, it is more to remind ourselves of Madam's expansive thinking.

Now we had reached the last night of the Leningrad season and the next morning we would be flying to Moscow. We, the stage management, technical and wardrobe staff, had the pack-up and get out to complete. In addition, the stage management were expected to go to all the Russian Heads of Department for a farewell drink of vodka. I could see that Martin Carr was faltering with the key into one of the pantechnicons so Leon Arnold, the Deputy Stage Manager, said I should go round the HODs as someone who was sober. So, I did and had a small glass of vodka with the Properties and Stage departments and thought nothing of it. Off I went to the electrics department which was based under the stage. As I approached, there was a gang of them at a trestle table, each one with a large bottle of vodka and pint-sized glasses. They rushed and grabbed me and poured a pint of raw(rogue) vodka down my throat. What I remember about that moment was running to the stage door to hug and kiss the gorgon outside, still in her Soviet army jacket, who was screaming, "Niet, niet ..." until one of the electricians pulled me away. Then I remember being carried back to the Astoria and ignobly up the shabby majestic staircase and being taken to my room, undressed and placed on the loo. Some kind person made sure I was up and somehow got on the plane.

The flight to Moscow was awful as I spent most of it upside down on the loo floor, apart from being fed slices of orange by Joyce Wells, the Wardrobe Mistress. Thank you, dear Joyce. Maybe if and when I reach the pearly gates, I can make contrition to you and all the Company's British and Russian staff for looking after me that night.

However, on reaching Moscow, we were then bussed to the Ukraine Hotel. That was another shaky journey for me. My room was on the 28th floor and the lift just zoomed up, even when I pressed frantically to get out.

I shouted Mushkoi (men's) or in cyrillic (if you can) with my hand over my mouth and found an aspidistra just in time, then returned to my room and passed out for 14 hours. I don't remember being reprimanded by anyone. A few days later, (or was it a dress rehearsal for the opening of the Moscow season?) I must have been checking dressing rooms and I came to Julia Farron. All she said was "Darling, all right now?" with a wry motherly smile and, "How do you feel now?" "Fine after 14 hours of sleep." "Never again?" she said. "Not with vodka," I replied, and I never touched it for over 30 years.

So, now we were in Moscow with the feel of summer but no longer in the warmth of spirit of Leningrad. Fortunately, before leaving Leningrad, the Company had requested that Alla must remain our principal interpreter for Moscow too. The four Muscovite ones - three young women and one young man - were certainly chosen by the Authorities and seemed to play the party lines. The Season opened with Frederick Ashton's 'Ondine' with, of course, the original cast of Margot Fonteyn, Michael Somes, Julia Farron and Alexander Grant. It seemed to be very well received. There followed two triple bill programmes. One day, sightseeing in Moscow, I had somehow wandered away from my companions and found myself amidst a surging crowd of Russian tourists obviously from across the Soviet (ex-czarist) "empire" for many seemed Mongolian. The crowd were getting increasingly excited. Forgetting the British Council strictures about our behaviour when in Russia, I set my camera at the ready. Some official rushed through the crowds to set up a carpeted platform with a couple of steps. A small little Russian blond boy was brought forward and a typical Russian embroidered hat was placed on his head. The crowd was getting increasingly excited. And then a great hush fell. Onto the platform climbed the summer-hatted chubby Papa Nikita Khrushchev, beaming all over. The little boy trotted up the steps and presented the bouquet that was larger than himself. Papa Nikita clasped the little fellow to his bosom, kissing him in the Russian style cheek to cheek - long before our footballers fell into this common place habit! So, I clicked my little camera, and I am still here. (If ever Madame Nina Khrushcheva, his granddaughter in New York, wishes to see the photo, she only has to contact me, but please, without any KGB.) Another day, (Sir) Frederick Ashton, Gerd Larsen one of the principal dancers and I had requested a visit to the historic monastery at Zagorsk, a bus ride again. On the way, we stopped on the roadside and I managed to click a photo of Gerd with some tiny smiling child wearing another embroidered little hat.

We arrived at the monastery and were taken for the official welcome by the Abbot. He was a very handsome man, finely robed with a very high black hat. Beside him sat a man in sandals and mismatched clothes who we were told was the Administrator. He seemed to us some KGB person and that the Abbot was either completely controlled or a fake. Afterwards, I made my way into one of the churches, standing at the back, and there to the left side, I saw a young woman looking across to the right side where there was a young man holding a baby. She seemed to give him a sign and he hastily baptised their baby - obviously - for there were no priests to do so.

Another day, we were taken by a rather fearsome interpreter by bus to see some Tchaikovsky museum. Sitting on the back seat were a few of the male leading principals. One of them, I think it was Alexander Grant, asked innocently, "Is there any homosexuality in Russia?" The interpreter vehemently replied in one short "NONE! (pause) Except in Georgia - and that is the fault of religion". Down came the guillotine! I suppose, in her mind, both Christianity and Islam were to blame.

For the end of the season at the Bolshoi, we pulled out all the stops and put on 'Sleeping Beauty' with Fonteyn and Somes, a performance with all guns blazing! For me, the two greatest ballerinas that I have seen in my life are Fonteyn and Ulanova. Of course, there have been so many others from London and around the world. Annette Page and Brian Shaw performed the Bluebirds' Pas de Deux, and before that, a glittering Florestan Pas de Trois with Merle Park, Donald MacLeary and Maryon Lane. When it came to the Bluebirds, the audience went ecstatic and really demanded an encore of Brian's solo. Jack Lanchbery, conducting, with theatre in his veins, raised his baton to Brian and they both took off, as did the audience - roaring. At its conclusion, Brian fell into the arms of stage management and was laid out flat in the prompt corner in a lake of sweat. The grand pas de deux was, to say the least, sublime.

We were coming to the end of this amazing experience of being in the USSR, but of course, there was a hitch. The charter flight that brought the dancers could not accommodate simply everybody. Madam, the Generalissimo/Commander, insisted that all the dancers had to return by the charter flight along with as many others as possible. So, she decided that she, Frederick Ashton, which did not please him, Martin the stage manager, me, Joe Kent the stage carpenter, the Chief Electrician and Jack Healy the Wardrobe Master would fly back on a scheduled flight. We were told that in any case, we would arrive back in London before the Company. We had to be at Moscow airport very early and there we remained for some 12 hours, and we saw the Company depart at 4.30. I think we were all in a very sombre mood. We were told to go to the restaurant and wait until some soup was served, which, on arrival, was spilt over Madam. She decided to sit outside reading her book - one by Dickens but the name of which I have since forgotten. Beyond the tarmac, there was a copse and Madam suggested I take Fred there. In the depths of the copse, there were some very hefty women in overalls and kerchiefs sawing wood. Fred grabbed my arm and said, "Take me back; this is awful." About 8 pm, a BEA rep came to us to say there was a plane to take us to East Berlin. So, we scrambled across to the plane we had been watching all day. A British Embassy official shoved a Sunday paper under my arm. Fred was first up the steps, then Madam got into her seat and had a coughing attack. I could only think of using the newspaper to fan in front of her. I opened it to see the headlines: "WORLD WAR THREE - Mass Exodus to the West!" We took off and I was glued to my window. We were flying so low that one felt one might touch the ground at any moment. All the way to East Berlin, we were flying above Warsaw Pact countries and the advancement of tanks, guns and armoury. In due course, we touched down somewhere outside East Berlin. We were handled by a very quiet and low-speaking air hostess who said we could still get across to West Berlin. She advised we should take the bus from where we were to Tempelhof and then a taxi to the Brandenburg Gate. So, we stood at the bus stop with a few countryfolk. Finally, the local bus arrived and suddenly, out popped the military - probably the infamous STASI. Our country companions rushed for the bus. Some were thrown out but fortunately, not us for we had all our luggage to load on.

We arrived at Tempelhof Airport which was surrounded by remains - nothing but the bomb site remains and weeds. Martin said to me, "Take Madam and Fred and your luggage and I will take the others and we will meet at the Kempinski Hotel". So, we took a lonely-looking taxi. Everything outside was very stark but the driver was very chatty. He pinched his jacket sleeve and said, "You see my coat? It is Communist clothes. No good. Nothing Communist good." Madam, cupping her hand but hardly with a stage whisper, said, "Don't speak to him; he may be a spy." Arriving at the Brandenburg Gate was the easiest part of the whole USSR escapade. The Russians were on duty at the gate and just waved us through. At the glorious Kempinski Hotel, we had accommodation courtesy of BEA. Obviously, Madam was in her element with all the men. She commanded again, "Let's meet in the bar". Joe Kent, the stage carpenter, was standing by. "He is bound to have ready cash, so we can have drinks on Joe." (He knew he would be reimbursed.) Apart from him, I don't think any of us had cash. We then sailed into a private dining room and had a delicious dinner with a dessert loaded with cream – well, in Deutschland - viele sahne. After dinner, Madam told Martin and me to go off into the night and explore West Berlin which was just light itself and with a sense of freedom. Just a few weeks later, the Berlin Wall went up. Thank God the Western Allies - America, Britain and France - stuck to protecting West Berlin, and indeed, West Germany. Alongside all of this international drama, of which we were completely oblivious, a superstar was jumping to freedom in Paris. Whilst in the USSR, we had been completely cut off from what was happening in the outside world so knew nothing about it. This superstar would affect the lives of all in the ballet world in some way or another for he was a phenomenon and a monster. Yes, unquestionably, he shook the stage.

Next day, the little band of warriors returned to London all in one piece. As Madam said to us over drinks, "We could be still stuck in Moscow or somewhere far away in Russia and never seen again."

Once back home, I went to see my parents, then it was back to the ROH to prepare for the new Season. Martin Carr told me that I was to learn the two new ballets for the triple bill, which may have been the opening programme of the season. One of the two was 'Jabez and the Devil' - music by Arnold Cooke, choreography by Alfred Rodriguez and designs by Isabel Lambert. The second was Kenneth MacMillan's new 'Diversions' with stage and costume designs by Philip Prowse. The staging was stark but completely stamped with classicism. This was a real success. Sadly, when revived in the early 70s on tour in the short-lived new group with excellent dancers that the ballet requires, Some of the classical elements of the decor were missing from the original production. This would not have pleased the designer.

Very soon after the opening of the season, the Stage Director told me I was going to be loaned to the Touring Company which had already started the Autumn Provincial Regional Tour to assist the newly promoted Stage Manager, Neville Pearson. His boss, John Healey, had transferred to Covent Garden to be the Chief Stage Manager of the Resident Royal Ballet. I had already made a few friends at the Garden so was rather miffed but hardly in a position to protest being at the bottom of the ladder.

Come Monday morning, off I set for Bournemouth. Neville Pearson was most welcoming, and we formed a good friendship professionally and personally. I quickly saw in that one week that this was where I must be with the Royal Ballet on tour. With eight performances a week for 12-week tours it would be bash, bash, bash, and onwards, so I would absorb the repertoire. Yes, I was instantly ambitious. So, Neville said I should speak to Mr John Field, the Director of the Touring Company, one of Madam's three directors.

I went to find him in the Company dressing room office. He was washing his "smalls" in the wash basin. This elegant man in black, with black-framed spectacles and dark brown eyes, looked at me as if I had just been released from some psychiatric ward. After a few seconds, he said, "Are you quite sure?" I replied, "I am absolutely sure". He added, "Life is not as comfortable on tour as in the Garden". So, I stayed for several years: it was my destiny.

The General Manager of the Royal Ballet at Covent Garden, Michael Wood, had an inimitable quiet and clipped voice seeming to come from lofty heights. Well, he was a very tall man and ex-Guards. He had brought Mark Bonham Carter, a member of the Ballet Subcommittee, to see the Company on tour. Michael was a dear and a real English gentleman. They came over to the prompt corner in the interval. Michael said in his clipped way, "This is the young man who wanted to remain on tour rather than return to the Garden. I think he must have gypsy blood in him." These were fun years, forever on the "road" around the United Kingdom and across Europe, especially in West Germany and across the world. In the UK, we would cover the major cities - Birmingham, Manchester, Leeds, Newcastle upon Tyne, and some of the larger towns such as Brighton. Usually, these tours were for 12 weeks but I remember one lasting for 17 weeks without a break which was very testing but somehow, with youth on one's side and "Dr Theatre", we kept going. Fortunately, John Field, the Director 0n Tour, was a Pied Piper who had a gift of rallying the dancers and all of us. On this tour, for me, such venues as Manchester Opera House were a new experience. Its Stage Manager was not exactly welcoming or helpful. As we headed northwards, we arrived in Newcastle upon Tyne at the Theatre Royal. I was able to stay with my parents – well, to sleep at least. I was able to arrange for my parents and two of their close friends to come to the Saturday evening performance of 'Les Deux Pigeons', Frederick Ashton's romantic ballet. My mother told me later that - perhaps being Welsh – my father's tears were frequent. Next morning, as I was leaving for the station to join all the Company on our Royal Ballet train, similar to the one in the USA though not exactly "Some Like it Hot", my father shuffled to the gate. He had been having frequent little strokes. He gave me a kind of Isaac blessing: "I now understand completely why you wanted to work in the theatre. I want you to know this now for we probably may not meet again". And he was right - over the gate was the last time I saw him.

So, we boarded our special train to Bonnie Scotland, travelling alongside the beautiful sandy beaches of Northumberland, across the Tweed and on into the majestic and historic city of Edinburgh, the Athens of the North. We then moved to the beautiful granite city of Aberdeen, and finally across to the rough and tough Glasgow, a city that was really alive. Those three Scottish cities were some of my favourites out of several across the United Kingdom. However, for audience response, warmth and enthusiasm, the best ones are Leeds, Liverpool, Newcastle upon Tyne and Bristol. I think we must have completed this UK tour, the first for me, in Scotland, after which we returned to London to prepare for our two-week Christmas/ New Year season in Monte Carlo at the Opera House of which the famous Casino was part. Although we were not allowed to work the gambling tables, we could wander around.

The repertoire for the season was 'Sleeping Beauty' with Margot Fonteyn and David Blair, and a triple bill of 'La Fête Étrange' with Elizabeth Anderton as La Chatelaine, and 'Beauty and the Beast' with David as the Beast. David, and Maryon Lane, his wife, and probably their twins, were staying in Anton Dolin's Monte Carlo villa and invited all the Company for a New Year's Eve celebration at which there was much after-performance dancing. Tito Arias seemed never to be off the dance floor with different partners. I remember perspiring so much from being on the dance floor that I decided to sit down. I looked up and there was Margot sitting right opposite me all alone and she said, "Come and talk to me, David". I know Princess Grace (Kelly) came to a performance to see Margot in 'Sleeping Beauty'. That must have been the occasion when Doreen Wells, Principal Dancer with the RB Touring Company and facially seeming so like Princess Grace, stood side by side and rather proved the point.

After ballet performances, some nights I would walk around the gambling tables in the Casino. It was fascinating to see the ancient women, highly made up, with long vermilion-painted nails/talons tapping on their chips whilst their eyes scanned the "talent" around the place. Possibly searching for a fifth husband or so? So-called marriage seemed to matter in those days.

During the day, once the performances were up and running, instead of the gambling tables, we took to the hall of fruit machines, and I won over £80. Yes - you guessed - I lost it all. Fortunately, some of my Puritan origins stopped further addictions, but I remain loyal to the whisky.

We returned to London to soon start another winter tour around the regions. I had planned to see my parents and family for a long weekend just before the tour and I managed to add another day to the weekend by delay. On one of these evenings, my father, whilst giving a lecture in Newcastle civic centre, had a stroke but was taken home safely. His doctor forbade him to leave his bed. He was known for being defiant. My brother John was called and told to stay the night with my mother. My father beat them both to the front door in the morning to collect the mail and his Times. In his thinking, only he was permitted to do so. He returned to his bed having defied his doctor, so my mother and brother waved my letter at him and said, "You see, David knows what he is doing. He will be up tomorrow having gained an extra day for the weekend". From his bed, he stretched his hand to my mother saying with his soft south Wales Welsh accent, "Sorry, Gwen, for the trouble I have given you in life". At that, the candle went out. I had missed it.

Demob party for Tony - Center front row with me on his left.

irov/Marinsky Opera House.

Alla, our chief interpreter in Leningrad & Moscow, June 1961.

Monica Mason (a future Director of Royal Ballet) leaving Lenin & Stalin Mausoleum, Red Square.

Senior dancers & children, and Sir Frederick Ashton on the bank bef
continuing to Zargorsk Monastery.

adam & the rest of us waiting at East Berlin bus stop.

The Defile for Madam with full company & School at Royal Opera Hous
Covent Garden October 1963.

3aalbek Festival, July 1965 - Royal Ballet with Fonteyn & Nureyev.

Sir Peter Daubeny greeting Impi Warrier - Umabatha World Theat
Season, April 1972.

So, back to London and we set off on another tour. I cannot remember the starting date or venue. Probably it was some Gaumont cinema, endlessly wide and shallow in depth - requiring the corps de ballet to be reduced from 8 to 6 swans per side. The show must go on at all costs - even by artistic standards, so, we bow to the Arts Council in order to get the grant! However, soon we would be moving to Stratford upon Avon for the Winter Season for 3 or 4 weeks. This was bliss with all the theatre facilities backstage enabling some new productions and revivals to be mounted despite the small stage – small, that is, for classical ballet. The Royal Shakespeare Company owned several properties around the town which many of us were only too happy to adopt and we took on a form of home life. However, many of the staff and dancers settled for the pubs with restaurants, especially the Dirty Duck and The Black Swan where many of the actors of the time were frequent visitors. Usually, as on this occasion, Stratford was followed by somewhere to "sober up" in every sense - emotionally, mentally and physically - to somewhere like Kingston upon Hull, which we called 'Hell Below Zero', with three dressing rooms - one small one as the Company Office and the other two large ones for the girls and boys respectively. Somehow, we did stage one of the famous Tchaikovsky ballets plus a triple bill. Mind you, I am describing things in the early 1960s and since then, a very fine regional theatre has been built to replace the 'Hell Below Zero'. On a subsequent visit in the mid-60s, there was the incident of the two white mice owned by one of the dancers, David Gordon from Ireland. The stage staff were somewhat suspicious, but the owner assured us that both mice were homosexual! Well, the next day, there was a terrible smell below stage. Lo and behold, in the mice's box were a dozen of the tiniest mice, the size of half of a thumbnail! The birth could have been a miracle and therefore sacred. So, either the mice, declared to be homosexual initially, were male and female, or one was bi-sexual. Maybe, on another occasion, one of the mice will be transgender.

Much of the rest of this tour has faded from memory, but I do remember it was great fun going in May to Belfast and Dublin. The train journey from Belfast to Ireland was hilarious in that the so-called Border and Customs Officers joined us in the compartment, just chatting, or, as the Irish say, having a real "craic". The real Guinness in both cities, I discovered, was like soft velvet slipping down the throat, especially in Dublin's historic and friendly pubs, accompanied by cold poached salmon and green salad.

The repertoire being presented at the Gaiety Theatre was 'Swan Lake', known then by its French title, and a triple bill comprising 'Les Sylphides' or 'Les Rendezvous' and two other ballets. The next day, we were preparing the triple bill programme. The Irish Chief Electrician, dressed in a dark navy suit just like all

Heads of Departments on both sides of the Irish Sea, was sitting on his chair down by the footlights. Addressing some other young electricians, he said, "Now, just look after the Englishmen properly," moving not an inch from his chair. "Now, why are you London folk looking so miserable?" The critic of the previous night's 'Swan Lake' had absolutely slated it, and especially "Madam", Dame Ninette de Valois, founder and director. We thought we would have been safe in Ireland as she was Irish. Of course, she was from that quite unique breed of Protestant Church of Ireland Anglo-Irish, many of whom lost their stately homes when they were burnt in the Irish Civil War. So, our Irish friend said, without moving, "You do not need to fuss yourselves about her (the Dublin critic); if she were in India, she'd be sacred!" It was another 40 years before I returned to both cities and other parts of the Emerald Isle with my Russian singers. Also, Ireland has changed dramatically since those days.

So, we returned to London to prepare for a London season at Covent Garden whilst the Resident Company would be on their American tour. For our season at Covent Garden, Frederick Ashton's 'Sylvia' was revised with Margot Fonteyn who had created the role. I think I am right in remembering that she was partnered by Brian Ashbridge, Flemming Flindt, a distinguished principal dancer from the Royal Danish Ballet, and Attilo Labis. Melissa Hayden from American Ballet

Theatre guested for two of the 'Sylvia' performances. I remember Flemming Flindt being such a pleasant person in this season.

After this season, which ended the ballet season for 1961/62, we must have had our annual holiday. Certainly, we were back in London in early September to prepare for our German and Scandinavian tour to Oslo, Stockholm, Hamburg, West Berlin and Copenhagen. The dancers who joined us from the Resident Company were Svetlana Beriosova and Donald MacLeary, Anya Linden (Lady Sainsbury), Lyn Seymour and Desmond Doyle. Shirley Graham had transferred from Covent Garden to the Touring Company as Principal Dancer. Ronald Emblen joined the Touring Company as a Principal previously in the London Festival Ballet. He and I became close friends until his death in 2003. He was a fine and inimitable Widow Simone in 'La Fille Mal Gardée'.

We started this tour in Oslo Opera House. Mostly what I remember was the whole Company being entertained on the beautiful boat Christianborg in Oslo Fjord, the brilliant blue sky and sunshine. Everywhere on deck seemed laid out with a delicious smorgasbord of seafood and drink! That must have been the day after the opening night. I think we must have gone on to Stockholm next, a beautifully clean city itself and the air around so fresh with water all around the city.

One day, we paid a visit to Drottningholm Palace Theatre, with all its advanced stage scenery and facilities for its time, yet dating back to the 17th century. From there, we must have gone on to Hamburg. Amongst other things, it was famous, especially to tourists, for women's mud wrestling. I remember Svetlana going, probably with Donald MacLeary. From Hamburg, we went on to West Berlin now the walled city. That is difficult for a visitor to imagine now. It was such a busy city with so many young Germans, many flown in from other parts of West Germany through the three flight corridord coming regularly from Hamburg in the north, Bonn/Koln from the west and Munich from the south. Undoubtedly, the resolve of the Western Alliance helped to save Western Germany and West Berlin, about 100 miles deep into East Germany, from the clutches of Stalin and the USSR by keeping the corridord to and from West Berlin alive. It was a tragedy that the USA and UK did not have similar resolve to insist in July/August 2022 with the Taliban that the US/UK would not remove their military services from Afghanistan until October in order to organise an orderly departure and avoid the tragedy that actually happened. History, no doubt, will not forget the reality.

So, from West Berlin, we travelled to Copenhagen to give about five performances at the Royal Opera House, home of the Royal Danish Ballet. The repertoire for this season was 'Sleeping Beauty' and a triple bill that included the dramatic ballet 'Checkmate', created in 1937 by Madam (Ninette de Valois) as the centre piece, with music by Arthur Bliss. Not surprisingly, Madam was much influenced by the threatening rise of Fascism and Nazism across Europe. On the opening night in Copenhagen, Neville and I split the calls to the dancers – half hour, quarter hour, 10 minutes and beginners. As I finished calling the quarter, I saw Madam on stage surveying the set. She spotted me and shouted, "Mossy (the Queen, also the Company Ballet Mistress) won't be seen; she's too far offstage". She flung back her black silk coat and stamped her foot and hooted, "I'll pull, and you push to my foot. Much better now, don't you see?" I could see her eyes would quickly go to the other side where the stools were set out for the Courtiers. I said, "We can stagger those." "Much better," she said. I happened to mention this was the Touring set. She screamed, "You should have come to your Director and I would have arranged for you to have the Covent Garden set." I replied, "The Garden set would be too big for the Copenhagen stage". "Well, never mind that. Come to your Director." That was that but not so. John Field escorted her through the pass door for the Prologue in the ballet. She was back on stage for the first interval and talking so much that the pass door was firmly shut and so she spent Act 1 in the prompt corner and said, "I will have to stay with you - much more fun..." and shrieked, "Tell me when you are getting busy. I will move out of your way." She chatted all the time. "Look at Svetlana's eyes; such beautiful eyes". Then, "Look at Donald's, such large dark brown eyes". "Madam, I am shortly going to get busy". It was coming to Carabosse's pricking of Aurora's finger and the wicked fairy's curse and transformation. I had just noticed that the gauze, in coming in, had fouled on a stage brace. I rushed there to disentangle it and there was Madam who screamed at me, "The gauze has fouled!" I hissed back, "I know, Madam." God help us, we had a new member of the stage! In the interval, I asked John to get Madam through to the audience as the next transformation of the Awakening scene was more complicated than the first.

The next morning, we were preparing the triple bill starting with 'Checkmate'. Having checked the lighting desk was set up as Madam would be truly prominent, I was about to open the pass door and there was Madam with John. I held the door back. She smiled at me and said, "Danke schön," and then said to John, "He's a charming German boy," despite having been with me in the prompt corner the previous night! A few days later, I went into the theatre canteen and there she was sitting laughing with a few of the boys (dancers) including Adrian Grater. They were into their cans of Tuborg beer. That fact had obviously escaped Madam. However, it was clear that she was enjoying something of an escape from Covent Garden! She too had known about touring life during World War II days when the Sadler's Wells Company was evacuated from London to the Northwest of England with two Pianists the inimitable Hilda Gaunt and the Music Director & Concuctor Constant Lambert.

A few days later, we all returned to London and the carousel of the autumn 12-week tour of the Regions, mostly the usual cities and towns, but including some others not so often visited, but done to pay our toll to the paymasters in order to keep the funding ongoing. In those days, there was one Arts Council of Great Britain. I think we finished in Blackpool in the large opera house which was appropriate for ballet. The general conditions backstage were great.

So, we came into the new year of 1963 and the endless winter. That was the Winter of Discontent for everybody. We were happy enough being stuck in the snow and ice in Stratford upon Avon, crossing southern England and being stuck in 9ft drifts on Salisbury Plain for many hours but most of us had prepared for this with supplies of flagons of wine and food. So, the shrieks of laughter rose ever higher, as did the smog from cigarette smoke. In those days, several dancers smoked at least 40 per day.

Eventually, we reached Taunton. Some of us stayed in the best pub in town. Of course, those of us who stayed there enjoyed a great welcome and so we lost much of our paltry salaries. The Monday night's performance of 'Swan Lake' had to be cancelled as the public could not reach the town. That winter, for 12 very long weeks, seemed endless. It must have been Cambridge next for the station was quite a way from the town centre and the Arts Theatre, too small really for ballet. Snow was just everywhere and falling non-stop. Trying to load all the scenery and costumes and being blinded by the falling snow was not fun and we were hoping that our train would reach the next date in time to fit up and open on the Monday night. At some point, we reached Brighton. The stony beach was covered in snow and the sea at the edges was absolutely iced, not just with a thin layer of ice. My digs had collapsed but what I found proved very interesting! Already installed were some of the pantomime boys. The owner arrived in two overcoats which she clung to, and I felt there was nothing else to keep her naked body warm. She turned out to be Mrs Emmet, wife of the strange designer who was often shown in Punch. I was sleeping in his room with all the strange machinery above my bed. I never met Mr Emmet. In the morning, I had a bath with a naked black man (china statue) leaning forward staring at me from between the hot and cold taps - rather disconcerting. Maybe the panto boys knew more about him. Eventually, we were freed from the snow, but I cannot remember much of that. Neville, the Stage Manager, gave notice as he was leaving to be Stage Manager at the soon-to-be-opened National Theatre in September under the directorship of Laurence Olivier with whom Neville had worked in Stratford. There was a spot for me in the Vic as DSM. When I discovered very soon that Bill Bundy was planning to engage someone from outside who had no knowledge of music even to just follow a score, meaning I would have to teach him all the repertoire, I went straight to John Field to protest. If this should be a fact, I was taking up the National Theatre offer straight away. "Leave it to me," he said. So, I was promoted more or less instantly. Much as I would have adored to work under Laurence Olivier's directorship, I believe I made the correct decision.

This brings us up to the new season in autumn 1963, both in the ROH and on tour. This started with The Dame Ninette de Valois' Grand Défilé on the Covent Garden stage arranged by Sir Frederick Ashton, her colleague for so many years, with the whole Company of dancers, Resident and Touring, Opera Ballet and the complete Royal Ballet School and the three Assistant Directors, Michael Somes, John Field and Michael Hart. The three stage bridges elevated and the whole Company processed in order of seniority ending up with the senior artists, Assistant Directors and Sir Frederick, now the Director, and finally the Star - MADAM - Dame Ninette de Valois. I think I was one of the four Stage Managers. Madam was in her spot ready to make her way to the last elevated stage and process to the front of the stage. Before setting off, she turned and said, "You need traffic lights for this job."

She was a handsome woman dressed full-length in pale blue with some little silver sparkles on the front.

I do not remember very much from that time, but I do recall the death of Doreen Wells' brother when we were playing the King's Theatre, Southsea. That night, she was the young love of the artist in the ballet 'Les Deux Pigeons' with particularly poignant music for Doreen, but, as a true professional, she got through the whole performance. Her tears were perfectly apporoporiate. The rest of the Autumn tour was the usual round of cities and towns in the Regions.

Then came 1964. We had another return to touring in Europe in late spring/early summer, mainly around Germany - West Berlin, Munich, Bremen, Osnabrück, Stuttgart - and the Holland Festival to Amsterdam, Rotterdam, Utrecht and Scheveningen. At the end of the Winter Regional tour, we came to Cardiff and were opening with 'La Fille Mal Gardée' as usual on Monday night, for which I had already booked a local pony. However, I, learnt my digs & pony were cancelled. I went off to pursue other digs passing entrance to Sophia Park was a big poster for Bertram Mills Circus opening the next night as the Royal Ballet. I passed the Sophia Park and noticed a great poster for Bertram Mills Circus opening the next night, Monday, the same night as the ballet. Hm... I must remember this....

A very large person opened the front door to me. She welcomed me in. I think she said £7 for the week with breakfast included in the price. In those days, theatre digs were a part of life for us tourers. Some digs' landladies were a special breed, particularly in Manchester, Glasgow, Leeds, and Liverpool, as they really could affect our life on tour over the years. My two favourites were Dolly Parrish in Leeds and dear Dorothy Kelly in Liverpool. Her two loves were Young Fr. Andrew and her theatrical guests. People such as Dame Edith Evans and Gwen Ffrancon Davies, Emlyn Williams and the Redgraves would only stay with Miss Kelly. I started off in the box room, and, a few years later, ended my last stay in the big brass bed with a huge crucifix that reached from the head of the bed to the ceiling.

So now, returning to Cardiff in the morning, my landlady arrived at the door of the box room with a large bang, bellowing basso profundo, "There's a woman in your room!" and delivered the cup of tea promptly at 7.45 am. So, having resolved the digs problem, I returned to see if the get-in at the theatre had been completed and Henry, the smoking and most loyal Ballet Master, had met his local extras (non-dancing) for the Monday night. So, we were now both free to withdraw to a nearby pub.

The pub was quite full except for a couple of high stools at the bar. We ordered our beers and were downing the first when I was nudged from my left side. There sat a strange little man with a bulbous nose who said, "I'm John the Baptist". "Well, I'm not your cousin," (Jesus)

I said. I'm not sure he was quite with me. Then he said, "I am the chef for Bertram Mills Circus." As he looked lonely and rather sad, I said, "Perhaps you can help me. Maybe the circus can help me with a pony." He replied, "Just ask for Fred at the entrance to the compound". "Thanks, my friend." The name didn't fool me but, in my situation, there was no time to think of pride! I had to find a replacement pony, or, at worst, I had to get Henry to provide two junior corps de ballet boys to pull the cart.

On my way from my digs on Monday morning, I went to the Circus Compound in Sophia Park and found two green buses which were being used as the telephone switchboard and general office, manned by two quite smart and equally South Kensington-accented people. "I've been told to ask for Fred," I explained. They both looked at me rather disdainfully and replied, "You mean, Mr Frederick Meredith. He is the Manager on tour." And so, I was taken to his presence. He looked quite the young officer material in manner and dress - military green and green wellies. So, he took me round the animals and the pen full of the most adorable white, blue-eyed Arabian ponies. That is how this one joined the Royal Ballet in Cardiff. Never before had the ballet had such a beautiful pony. Of course, the pony was nearly the star of the show. Frederick invited me to come to the circus later in the week and that was the start of a good friendship. On the Wednesday night, I was able to get away and take Brenda Last with me. Afterwards, we went to his 2-levelled large caravan all painted in pale green with some beautifully hand-painted pictures of Coco the Clown, the Circus's star clown. Whilst there, I met Norman Barrett, tall and elegant in his red tailcoat and silk top hat. Over the years, Frederick and Noman became good friends and I would join them as I did the Christmas/New Year in '64. Circus life is very disciplined. Call sheets for the next day's calls/rehearsals are posted the evening before at the end of the last performance, with the first call in the ring at 7.00 am - maybe the trapeze or whatever. One time, I joined a small group, I think with Norman, in one of the caravans and different artists from across Europe who hadn't seen one another for a few years. Although they were drinking to celebrate, none of them seemed to be heavy drinkers – well, they couldn't afford to be. Norman had introduced me to his mother, Mrs Barrett, a little gentle lady who drove one of the very heavy trucks along with the rest of the gang. Yes, circus folk are also a special breed, as are dancers.

After finding a new pony via Bertram Mills in Cardiff we had another return to touring in Europe in late spring/early summer, mainly around Germany - West Berlin, Munich, Bremen, Osnabrück, Stuttgart - and the Holland Festival to Amsterdam, Rotterdam, Utrecht and Scheveningen.

In Mid Summer 1965 with a reduced size Ballet Company went to the Menotti Spoleto Festiva in Italy to mount Rudolf Nureyev's production 'Raymonda', with music by Glazunov and designs and costumes by Beni Montresor, with Margot Fonteyn and Nureyev in the leads. I was the Stage Manager but deprived of all our normal staff. Fortunately, the Italian Festival staff were excellent. However, it was quite dramatic getting the ballet launched. I decided to go into the theatre early on the morning of the "generali" (dress rehearsal) to which the film studios and aficionados and Menotti's friends, including Leonard Bernstein, were coming. I wanted to go through my production score in the empty theatre so I could talk to myself in the prompt corner. I started when suddenly I heard a small voice saying, "Somebody else, like me, has come so early to be in the silence of the place," followed by a little titter. Of course, it was Margot, piecing and placing her head dress as with her quiet thoughts on the ballet. Shortly afterwards, Joan Thring, Nureyev's agent at the time, came rushing to me saying, "Where's John Field?" "Not here yet - too early". "It's Margot, she's taken a taxi to Fiumicino Airport to get to Panama." Tito, her husband, had been shot a few weeks before and lead poisoning had travelled into his blood stream. Soon afterwards, Menotti arrived in despair crying, "My Festival is ruined!" All I could say was, "John Field has Doreen Wells well-rehearsed for the role ready for any disasters." Not much consolation, I know. Doreen danced all of the Spoleto performances and naturally gained great public acclamation.

Strange to say, at one of the latter full dress rehearsals, Margot was checking the stage when she spied three little posies of flowers made from real live flowers from the fields which the Italian prop master had organised. The posies would be placed by Raymonda's friends diagonally across the stage. She rushed to me to have them replaced by artificial ones. She cried, "There will be a disaster otherwise". And so there was. I remember when I started in weekly rep in Newcastle, real flowers could never be used on stage; this was a superstition across theatre land in this country.

Margot did return and continued with the Company to the Baalbek Festival with Rudolf and his Raymonda plus a triple bill that included Robert Helpmann's 'Hamlet' with Rudolf as the title and Margot as Ophelia.

Baalbek was an amazing experience, certainly before the Lebanese Civil War. The site itself was and, hopefully, is again, breathtaking. The electrician, Alec, could not light the ballets until dark so late in the night under a clear and brightly starred sky. The switchboard was set on top of a high pillar climbed by a rickety wooden ladder. The wind, which had gathered strength, had seemed to shake the whole platform. To start with, I am nervous of heights. To descend I made young Hasan descend immediately ahead of me. It was pitch black. I was cautiously finding and placing my steps on the uneven ladder rungs until safely back on terra firma.

On one of our free daytimes, Johaar Mosoval invited me plus three of the girls and Farley Richard, one of the Principals, to a Sheik's encampment on one of the plains either just inside Syria or very close in Lebanon. We had a hair-raising switchback drive there. We were thrown into the midst of all these male blue-eyed Arabs who sat all around the Sheik's huge tent and stared at us. The Sheik clapped his hands for cushions for Johaar to sit by him like his consort. Then he clapped again for his two wives, one with a small dagger in her hand who then came back with a sheep whose neck she stuck the dagger into. The sheep was our banquet! The men started drinking and the heat was rising fast. We, the visitors, stayed clear of arak, a white spirit. The Arabs were getting randy. It was quite apparent they were attracted to the one young blonde girl and also to Richard Farley. He expressed some nervousness to me. I told him, "Don't move around, just sit still." I felt we might not get back for the evening performance so said we had to all leave for rehearsals. The return journey to Baalbek was even more switchback and threatening than the earlier one, however, we made it. A few days later, we returned to London and our annual holiday.

After that, we regrouped to prepare for our new 65/66 season of touring the Regions and the Covent Garden Season whilst the Resident Company would be in the States in the summer months. This included the Royal Ballet School Saturday matinee performance followed by the Touring Company's performance of 'Swan Lake'. The following week, The School's matinee performance of 'The Two Pigeons' transferred for a week at Holland Park open-air theatre.

Soon afterwards, we were all off on holiday and hopefully refreshed for a return to an Autumn Regional tour again. I remember that one of the new dancers to join the Touring Company was Nicholas Johnson, just 18. He had been the gypsy lover in 'The Two Pigeons' at the School Matinee in Holland Park. He was always full of energy and vitality then and, indeed, ever after in his career. He was a very fine artist and dancer, both in the Royal Ballet and later with the London Festival Ballet.

In 1967, Vernon Clark, the Touring Company Manager, transferred to the Resident Company at Covent Garden. John Field asked me to remain the Stage Manager as well as Company Manager. I knew that early, and through summer 1968, the Company would be on a hectic and heavy West European zig-zagging tour which it certainly proved to be. I was most fortunate that Judith Nicholls was the secretary and very supportive of the new young Company Manager and has remained a great friend ever since. At this time, I moved from my one room in the Ballet Mistress's Chelsea flat where I had been since 1962, to share Keith Grant's Pimlico flat. He was the young General Manager of the Royal Opera. For me, it was a good arrangement as we were usually in performance on alternate nights. In those days, Pimlico seemed to provide a distinct locality with a corner shop. It was pleasant for the two of us walking all the way to the Royal Opera House crossing St James' Park and the Mall. Yes, Central London was less bursting at the seams than now. Or is it that age does jade one somewhat? I remember that Keith gave me a real welcome by serving his home-cooked moules marinière - delicious.

So, we come to 1968 and the European tour with Margot Fonteyn and Rudolf Nureyev the two main stars. However, we actually began in the May in Bordeaux, right in the heat of the student and anti-de Gaulle riots. The Company was booked into several hotels when the circumstances were such that it would have been better if we were in just one. John Field and I were in Le Grand Hotel directly opposite the theatre. My room was also the office with a huge fridge full of booze which proved most useful. I and Henry Legerton, the Ballet Master, escorted Mrs Barrett who was in charge of the pigeons for 'The Two Pigeons' performances. The auditorium was festooned with red flags and besieged by the students. This was the era of the leftist student movement. We returned to our hotels with Mrs Barrett and her feathered couple. The real fun would start towards midnight. John and I had a grandstand view from the balcony onto "la Place". The flag stones were torn up for battle with the Prefecteur de police trying to calm down the ugly scene to no avail. The crowd would pick him up and throw him down with the gendarmes and military getting rough. So, no performances took place and, for a few days, we were confined to the hotel. Lies Askonas, our agent for this date, who was a great friend of the Rothschilds, would return to us from their estate loaded with strawberries and cherries and some champagne. The only means of contact with London was via the wall phone in my room. One day, John Tooley put a call through. John Field was just popping another bottle of champagne. “What was that?” asked John Tooley anxiously. John said, “Just another gunshot”! Finally, we did get back to London by French Airforce plane leaving at about 4 am in order to dodge any public disorder. Before we left, I had to round up the company in the other hotels to make sure they were ready for leaving. I discovered that some senior dancers were in a misty den of “vice” and smoke and pot and iniquity! I threatened them with rape, etc., but I just got the two fingers. We landed via the French Airforce in London all in one piece. It was then a turn around to the next date of the West European tour which I think was Wiesbaden, which certainly was on the tour where Fonteyn and Nureyev joined us. Immediately preceding us was the Kirov Ballet who, at their last performance preceding our opening one, slipped in ‘Le Corsaire’ with their famous dancer, Yuri Soleviev, a contemporary of Rudolf in the Kirov Ballet. It was also one of Rudolf’s most famous pas de deux with Margot. I went to check the posters outside the theatre and saw that a rather crude addition with Soleviev's name had been added. Leaving the area, I glimpsed Nureyev just leaving and it was obvious that he had noticed too. Well, when it came to our opening night, Rudolf's performance was absolutely electric. Every time he rounded the stage, he seemed to be shouting out, "FUCK, FUCK, FUCK". His language was often colourful!

In those days, and before entering the Common Market, there were all the different currencies that I could never close down because of the zigzagging of the tour. I already had my shabby touring bag for cash full of all the different currencise which never left me. A soloist and her husband had already labelled me Herr Zloty Meister and that I remained for the rest of my time with the Company. We were flying with Spantax Airlines, rather second rate with bumpy flights and landings, which was quickly nicknamed 'Tampax'.

We progressed to the south in Portugal where I remember eating excellent food and drinking white wine in a very elegant restaurant that proved to be a smart brothel, I think for both sexes, seeing some of the very junior staff who looked suspiciously underage. Portugal at the time was a fascist state, as was Spain, where we reached in a zigzag way. Madrid was an imperial and historical city under the fading grip of Franco. It was now real summer and getting very hot for us delicate folk from the North! Santander, Barcelona and Valencia were all on our touring agenda. In Valencia, some of us went to a bullfight where Margot's dressing room was next door to the bull's room! She thought it great fun hearing him snorting next door! It was my first and only visit to a bullfight and will remain the only one.

We also went on to the municipality of Lorca for a couple of performances of 'Giselle' in the Granada Festival at the Generalife, close to Alhambra Palace in which hotel I was staying and where I found, delivered in my name to my room, a supply of extra stage lamps! On the opening night, there had been crowds of press with telescopic lenses closing in on the stage. I warned our impresario for some of the tour, Julian Braunsweig, - also joint founder with Dame Alicia Markova and Anton Dolin of London Festival Ballet - that he must get this mafia stopped otherwise Margot particularly would stop the performance of 'Giselle'. "Yes, yes, I do some things". I could see these pressmen getting ever closer to the orchestra and one hanging over the orchestra barrier with a telescopic lens ready to pounce. The orchestra started, the corps de ballet entered and Margot started dancing and suddenly stopped and shouted that she would not go on. I flew to the scene, pushing away the pair of feet on the front row whilst I grabbed the photographer by the back of his trousers. Whether in consequence or not, who knows, but his expensive telescopic camera was smashed. When so-called calm was restored, Rudolf stepped forward and said to the conductor, "And faster next time." Before the performance started, I had told Judith, my secretary, and Erling, the ballet teacher, as they were going to the bar, to have a large gin and tonic ready for me when I joined them after the performance. There they were sitting on the bar's balcony with a view directly towards the Sierra Nevada. The large G & T and the heavenly nighttime view restored me from a rather fraught evening at the ballet. Close by at the bar was a group of attractive young men and women around my own age, smartly and suitably dressed on a hot summer's night. One of them came to me and said, "Oh, His Highness is sorry his feet were in the way and would like to buy you a drink!" Not minding being sent up, I said, "Yes, please, another gin and tonic, thanks". My host later was proclaimed the restored young King of Spain!

We were drawing to the end of a long and arduous tour but still had Monte Carlo and the Nervi Festival to visit. Monte Carlo was great fun and after the performance, the Palace had invited all the Principal dancers, including me, to a cold supper beside the handsome pool. It was another joyful ballet night joined by gracious and fun-loving Princess Grace and Margot and Rudolf! But I could not get out of my evening suit as "*wherever the Zloty Meister went, the zlotys had to go too!*" So, I had to stuff all the French francs into all my pockets which was just as well. All the Principals, except Lucette Aldous in her evening frock and I, were already in the pool. I took to one of the children's boats and helped Lucette into the boat with me. Rudolf and a couple of other dancers spied us sedately rowing, fortunately, close to the side of the pool, and swam over and tipped the boat over and we went glug, glug, down. Once I was upright, dripping, one of the Prince's aides came to me to say that the Prince wished the party to finish and everybody to leave the pool. So, I had to round up all the dancers. Hence I, and Lucette, who was not amused, dripped across the courtyard and out of the Palace entrance down the streets back to the hotel. After I had stripped down, I set out all the wet francs from my wet zloty bag on the balcony and covered everything with a sheet from the bed which I hardly needed for just the few hours' sleep I would get. Whether Nervi Festival was the next date I am not sure, but John Tooley called me to tell me that I should collect a large supply of lira again in hard cash from the recent visit of the English Opera Group. So, when we finished this long tour, I had the equivalent of £30,000 of hard cash in open currencies in my shabby grimy zloty bag. When we arrived back at Gatwick on Spantax/Tampax Airlines, John Field said, "After surviving this tour, John Tooley owes us a taxi all the way to London". I replied something like, "I think we can afford that." I asked John to guard my zloty bag whilst I changed some cash into sterling. When I turned round, there was the zloty bag all alone. John was strolling towards me and screaming, "Where've you been, taking so long?" I said, "Where's the bag?" John blanched and we bundled ourselves into the car and laughed much of the way back to London.

Soon afterwards came happy holidays, after which another Autumn Regional tour then 1964 would begin in Stratford upon Avon. Here, Geoffrey Cauley created his first ballet for the Company, 'In The Beginning', to Poulenc's Oboe and Clarinet Sonatas - very haunting and mood music. The cast of Alfreda Thorogood, David Wall, Lucette Aldous and Kerrison Cooke... all I can say is a very beautiful little ballet.

The highlight of this year was probably the Cairo Festival in Giza, near the Pyramids in early September. We arrived late at Cairo airport. On the flight to Cairo, I told the Company that we would find the climate quite extreme for us and they should be sensible around midday, especially knowing how much dancers liked swimming pools as swimming is the one exercise they can safely take. The Company's new secretary, Claire Thornton, had just joined me from working at Covent Garden. As we were so late, I told Claire she better go with the Company directly to the recently reopened Mena House Hotel in Giza, just a short walk to the Pyramids and the site where the Company would dance with the Sphynx as the actual prompt corner and some vast tablet of rock from ancient times as their backcloth. Maggie Fox and I had to remain in customs until she got clearance for all the pointe and ballet shoes for the week's performances, and I, yet again, for lighting equipment. By the time Foxie, as she was always called, and I arrived at the hotel in the early hours, under a hugely starry clear night sky, the Company were all checked in. They had rushed into the depths of the desert. Some had already found Memphis. I slept for a few hours then was ready with Claire to work out everybody's subsistence allowance in the Company office - my suite - which had been Winston Churchill's during WW2. John Field, as Director, was allocated General Montgomery's suite. My phone rang and it was the Stage Manager, Jeffrey Phillips, saying that Maggie Fox had collapsed in the pool. "You are all so silly jumping into the pool at midday in the height of the heat," I retorted and went back to the counting house. The two senior dancers, very good friends of mine, called me to say that they had carried Foxie from the pool to the swimming pool attendant who was also the hotel masseur and was trying to resuscitate her. But this was serious. I got the hotel staff to call for medical help but she was dead. It all became ghoulish. A macabre funeral hearse arrived with black and silver tassels and so I went off with it into a Cairo morgue. The British Council's Director of Dance and Drama, who had been very responsible for getting us to the Festival, came with me. This procedure continued for several days. Meanwhile, our performances of 'Swan Lake' and the triple bill proceeded though the Company were in a sombre state when offstage. On the last of my daily morning visits to the Cairo morgue, through chaotic and terrifying traffic and accompanied by Jane, the BC rep who was flying back to London with the leaded coffin to check through customs our end, I noticed a little old lady with big black eyes sitting on a little chair under a leafy tree, staring at me. Suddenly, two men rushed out of the morgue carrying a small bundle of sacking between them. It brushed against me, and I saw the smashed-in face of a small child. That and the heat just flipped me. But suddenly, the little old lady was beside me with her little chair and took me to the tree. Then we had to go through the customs sealing and off went Jane and Foxie to Cairo airport, then to London and finally to rest. By the time I reached Giza, it was night and the performance had started. With no food and trudging knee-deep into the sand everywhere, I joined John in watching the performance. He turned to Geoffrey Cauley who was with him and said, "Get him a large G and T with ice". It saved me. But apart from the sadness, we did have several laughs and returned better for the visit. What I learnt and valued was the great kindness of the Egyptians, especially at the hotel. Everybody wanted to respect different customs and Christian traditions. But it was difficult for me to appreciate the wailing women at the morgue and Cairo cemetery.

So, back to London and off on another Autumn Regional tour. During this autumn tour, we returned to Scotland, and, for me, what was memorable during our

DALTA (Dramatic and Lyric Theatre) season in Glasgow was that I was able to go to the Citizen's Theatre to see Tennessee Williams' 'The Milk Train Doesn't Stop Here Anymore' with Constance Cummings, designed by Philip Prowse, one of the Triumvirate Directors of the Theatre. It was a fabulous production. The following year, 1970, (for the last time with the Ballet) when back in Glasgow on a night off, I went to the Citizens' Studio Theatre to see 'Tis a Pity She's a Whore' designed by Philip, and stunning it looked in the simplest of ways. It started with organ music and a huge wooden chandelier full of lit candles suspended to stage level. Then the play starts with the chandelier raised to a preset level as the organ music fades away. The walls of the studio were painted completely in a khaki colour which evoked the period of the play. This was, for me, another special experience. Over 30 years, the Citizens was to continue to produce such innovative work.

We finished this tour in December at The Grand Theatre Leeds. Here, Geoffrey Cauley created 'Lazarus' with Elizabeth Anderton as Mary Magdalene and Ronald Emblen as Lazarus and with Geoffrey's own white designs which became a Cauley feature.

Later in the Summer Season at the Garden, Madam's 'Job' was revived after many years, with Kerrison Cooke as Job. I remember those stage rehearsals. It must have been the piano dress rehearsal and Sir Adrian Boult was in attendance. I met him at the stage door to take him to the orchestra pit. Madam arrived from the Underground looking grim and wearing a turban as if from an air raid shelter, one of the ends of the turban facing upwards and the other end facing downwards, rather like my father's red eyebrows when a student was being rushed into his study to have his prepared sermon dissected! So, I could tell in advance that this piano dress rehearsal was going to be lively. Madam's target was God, way up at the back of the stage. On a certain point in the music, (Ralph Vaughan Williams) God gets up. This morning, he found himself up & down endlessly. Madam would shout out, "STOP! You are not on the music." This went on several times. Finally, Madam shouted, "STOP – God, get it right." Sir Adrian, with his head just seen above the orchestra barrier, said quite gently, "Dame Ninette," Dame Ninette," but Madam was too intent on God getting it right, until Joy Newton, her aide de camp, managed to get Madam's attention that Sir Adrian was calling her. Madam instantly became quite skittish and rushed down to the orchestra pit. Sir Adrian, with a voice as if from a lofty height, said, "Dame Ninette, I do wish I could talk to God like you do". Of course, she blustered, "Oh, Sir Adrian," and laughed. I do not remember much else of that morning other than I collected Sir Adrian and took him to the stage door and the waiting car.

Soon after, The Royal Ballet Touring Company ended its life in Wimbledon with 'Swan Lake' - a sad and apposite finale - a performance appropriately poignant and vigorous and true to the spirit of the Company. Lucette Aldous was not remaining in the Company who had given such stalwart service to the Royal Ballet as she had done previously in London Festival Ballet. Of course, she was quickly absorbed by Australian Ballet and Nureyev instantly chose her to be his partner in his new production of 'Don Quixote' for the Company. I remained with the Company as Company Manager of the newly formed unit, The New Group, to tour the Regions with a reduced basic company and principal/soloist dancers shuttling weekly from Covent Garden to wherever we were on tour in specific ballets. This included a new ballet, 'Field Figures' by Glen Tetley, with contemporary music by the German composer Henze. This really was a great new experience choreographically and musically but not exactly for the tastes of the Regions. Also, we had 'Checkpoint' by Kenneth MacMillan, set to contemporary music. Later in the winter, I went with the Company's The New Group to Stratford upon Avon for the last time. Whilst there, I decided I would leave the Royal Ballet at the end of the RB's Sadler's Wells 3-week season in July. I blithely told some RSC management that should they be looking for cloakroom staff, I could be available. They laughed. Actually, I meant what I said as I had no future plans set up. After waiting at home for three weeks, the phone rang and it was Robert Vaughan, the theatre manager at Stratford on Avon, who had just learnt of my very recent departure from Covent Garden.

Part 4

His first words were, "Dai bach, are you free?" I said, "What do you mean? You thought I was joking last February." He wanted me to help him as House Manager for a few weeks until the one who had been engaged would be free to join. So, off I went with Pearl, my companion, the cat. Bob provided me with one of the theatre's several properties diagonally opposite the theatre. Pearl was perfectly happy with the garden at the back of the cottage as there were runner beans and stalks she could climb. When on the Royal Ballet Winter annual seasons, I met and got to know the front-of-house staff who were jolly and so helpful. It was a useful short experience. A highlight was being able to see so many performances of Peter Brook's stunning production of 'A Midsummer Night's Dream'. One realized and felt that a revolution had taken place, certainly in British Theatre, and indeed, an influence across the globe. Yes, Peter Brook was a true Guru. But he had already proved his genius as the 21-year-old Director of Opera at Covent Garden shortly after the end of WWII. Bob Vaughan told me he would be going on holiday shortly and would then be working on his antiquarian book business for a further few weeks and would like me to deputise as Theatre Manager. I was cautious about getting over-committed to Stratford as I wanted to get back to London, not that I had anything on offer. John Field, having left the Royal Ballet, would be taking up directorship of the Ballet at La Scala, Milan and would want me to manage the Piccola Scala when used by the ballet. Meanwhile, David Brierley, General Administrator of RSC, asked me about my future plans with John Field. As there was nothing to report, he offered me the job of managing the new RSC's forthcoming Autumn studio season at the Place - London Contemporary Theatre. The RSC were building a 3-sided studio within this very large dance studio which would be totally destroyed at the end of the season.

I must say it was a very exciting project. It opened with Trevor Griffiths' 'Occupations' with Patrick Stewart as Lenin, Estelle Kohler as the Baroness and Ben Kingsley as Gramsci, the Italian Communist. The knockout farce and premiere was 'Section Nine' about a US American special intelligence Unit with the superb Colin Blakely and Margaret Whiting, his wife, and indeed, the rest of the male cast. It was full of hilarious lines with one delivered by Colin addressing his unit, "Your weapon is your cock," and seemed to be holding one. I suppose by today's standards, it could seem rather corny. It pulled the crowds in. The public were desperate to see the show and I had to hold letting the performances start as I packed in the extra bodies whilst asking the audience to move ever closer to each other. It really was an intimate show! However, audiences seemed very willing to help, what with it being a laugh a minute. It was the triumph yet it was never repeated after the season. I cannot remember press reviews but likely some would have been critical. The other great hit in this season was Strindberg's 'Miss Julie', with a stunning performances by the young Helen Mirren, Donal McCann and Heather Canning.

Just after this season, David Brierley called me again at midnight asking me to help get Peter Daubeny off his back. When was David (Brierley) going to find him a liaison officer for his forthcoming World Theatre Season opening in early April in the Aldwych Theatre? I had, before leaving the Royal Ballet, written to Peter but did not receive a reply. I learnt through working with him how punctilious he was on replying to all correspondence. I discovered later that my letter was received but never reached Peter. Obviously, I said yes to David B. This began a very happy time in my life of theatre, in which, I felt by the end, I could spend the rest of my working life in this niche & atmosphere. I worked closely with the local Aldwych technical staff. Most were cockneys and rogues, but I forged a real link, especially with Alfred Davies who was a great admirer of Peter Daubeny. Perhaps seeing Peter in a mohair coat encouraged Alf to have one. He really could perform a miracle to get a difficult production onto the stage for the Monday night - the Companies having just arrived on the Sunday afternoon with no allowance for any delays. Mind you, that was the same in my time with the Royal Ballet - arrive Sunday, open Monday. So, with my first experience at the Aldwych, we nearly did not open for Alfie had to cut into the stage forefront to reset the trampoline for Lorca's 'Yerma' with wonderful Núria Espert and her splendid company. The show was lit over the performance and then relit the following morning. Remember, Spain was still under Franco's dictatorship. Censorship had refused the final scene when the trampoline was raised revealing all the company completely naked in hell. It was so exhilarating. Peter insisted it must be so in London and it was. 'Yerma' was preceded by the Natal Theatre Workshop Zulu Company, a Zulu version of Macbeth. Remember, the Apartheid Government was in power, so it was politically difficult to negotiate. Peter's wife, Molly being originally from South Africa, was very important in these negotiations. And indeed, she played a most important role in the life of the seasons over the years. She added glamour and was a natural "grande hôtesse" at a political level, as well as in the theatre internationally and in London. The Zulus were triumphant. There was the wonderful moment when the Impis advanced, a troop zooming down from the back of the stage with bass shouts. The audience responded orgasmically, and it felt as if the Aldwych roof had been lifted upwards. Four other eminent Companies also took part.

For my blank autumn period and without any RSC salary, I had to think quickly. I suggested to David Brierley, the RSC General Administrator, that I should go as the Advance Manager for the whole tour with my experience of touring across the globe as I could tell where there could be complications. David agreed. The RSC, supported by the British Council, were sending the amazing Peter Brook's 'Midsummer Night's Dream' on a European tour starting in Paris and performing at the Sarah Bernhardt Theatre, later to be renamed Le Théâtre de la Ville. The other western Europe date was at Teatro La Fenice in Venice, an opera house and not ideal venue for Peter Brook's production and Sally Jacob's distinctive costumes. From there, we went to Eastern Europe which was a very special experience, especially the response of the young and the students. I would go ahead of the Company to all the different countries. From Venice, Belgrade was the first and easiest, then I think we must have gone to Zagreb. I know I was there on 2nd November (All Soul's Night). Either the Cultural Counsellor or one of the Embassy staff took me to this big cemetery, on a large hill overlooking the city, covered in deep fog. I was aware of candles moving around in the dark and cold fog. Sometimes, one touched other bodies in this eeriness. Yugoslavia was very straight forward compared to the rest of Eastern Europe. We must have gone from Zagreb to Budapest - Buda looking down on Pest - but one city. One night, after my supper and decent wine, I noticed the name of our hotel. At the reception desk, there was a line-up of young men and I asked them what 'Schabazar' meant. (Hungarian friends, forgive my attempt at the word and spelling!). They all, in a line, raised their arms sideways and with a big smile and laughing said, "It means Freedom!" The next day, I must have left for Bucharest which was quite a shock with its pitiable poverty and sadness. I had one meal at the one restaurant in the city, the Bucharesti. We had some devoted interpreters from student level. There was Lilla and the young doctor. Lilla had a fiancé who had already managed to get out to Copenhagen. I remember Alan Howard saying, "Come on, David, do your stuff; marry Lilla (marriage of convenience) so that she can get to Copenhagen." This was set up at the British Embassy for the next morning before I would be catching the Red Star train from Moscow to Sofia, Bulgaria via Bucharest, but dear Lilla was not seen again.

Before we left London, we had a stage basket crammed with the leftover beautiful Peter Brook programmes from the Stratford season as handouts to all students who came in their droves along the tour. In these programmes was a special dedication from himself that this production was all to do with liberty and freedom of speech and words, etc. Before leaving London, we were given a pep talk that we must not be involved in any propaganda or circulating leaflets of any kind. Every opening night in the Eastern Bloc was filled with the Communist party and apparatchik. So, Hal Rodgers, the Company Manager and Stage Manager, me and the British staff pulled students in through the backstage windows and piled them into the unused orchestra pit and placed as many of them around the sides of the stage as we could, handing all of them a dedicated Peter Brook programme. This also happened in Sofia and Warsaw. These students had texts of the Dream and would quote easily. Bulgaria was the most orthodox of the Warsaw Pact countries and Poland the least for the Poles are the freest in spirit.

I went on to Warsaw and was graciously received by the Cultural Attaché and invited to dinner at his home. After dinner, I was taken to the library for whisky. I was ready for this as I had been quite abstemious on this tour. After toasting, he said, "And about these special programmes you have brought with you... One of the Company actresses said joyfully that you gave away Peter Brook's special programmes to all the students in Bucharest. It seems she had drunk perhaps a little too much!" I, of course, said that I knew nothing of this at all - lying for a most worthy cause. However, one of our own technical staff opened another stage basket and found it crammed full of Moral Rearmament pamphlets! 1972 ended fascinatingly and successfully.

In the New Year, I would be joining up again with Peter and Molly Daubeny for the final World Theatre Season. As Peter's health was beginning to fail, he asked me to be his new PA and manager of the 1973 season. But before starting, I had agreed to being one of the small team to manage several small programmes, for the celebration of the United Kingdom's entry into the European Community. Then it was back to work with the World Theatre Season. Mine was English Romantics with Richard Pasco and Barbara Leigh in Lincoln's Inn, The Chieftains from Ireland, some jazz concerts and a couple of painting exhibitions, one being the famous Dutch painter, Aelbert Cuyp. Then I took 10 days holiday in Tunisia staying in a hotel with a room opening onto a swimming pool, and, through an orange grove, straight onto the beach. Then it was back to wads Square and the hub of the WTS work.

There were eleven Companies in all from the 1972 season, and others from previous seasons. I remember distinctly the Burg Theater from Vienna with Schnitzler's 'Liebelei'. Again, such a disciplined company and perfect ensemble acting. Of course, it was special for me to see the Royal Dramatic Theatre from Stockholm with Ingmar

Bergman's acclaimed production of 'The Wild Duck'. The season finished with the return of 'Umabatta' and the Zulus who had rocked audiences in 1972.

In the autumn of 1973 and '74, I returned to the RSC at The Place. What I remember particularly is Athol Fugard's 'Hello and Goodbye' with Janet Suzman, and Ben Kingsley as her brother, depicting two poor white people, especially in the poignant scene of Janet having to go through the clothing of her dead mother.

In June 1973, Peter Daubeny was knighted. He came to occasional performances only as he was weakening.

By now, Peter was too ill to be involved in working. One morning, I entered the Daubney's Chelsea home as Molly (Lady Daubeny) was coming down the stairs. She asked me if I would help her make the last few months the happiest we could. So, plans were started for a mini-World Theatre Season 1975 comprising three Companies that Peter had already chosen: the Gothenburg Swedish Theatre and the Kraków Stary Teatr, again with Andrzej Wejda and his production of 'November Night' at the Aldwych, and the next week, with Konrad Swinarski's production of 'Forefather's Eve' (Djadi) in Southwark Cathedral. Molly went to see it in Kraków and returned saying how amazing it was but probably impossible to present. The Polish authorities passed it to come believing that we would react negatively. I suggested through her connection with the Polish Ambassador that we should get the

Director over and I would take him to the Aldwych Theatre and have him explain the story line. I quickly saw that it could never really work in a theatre. It needed ideally to be in the space of a church. So, we walked over to the Actor's Church, St Paul's in Covent Garden. I knew they could not offer us a week, so we took a taxi to St. John's, Smith's Square, a de-sanctified church that presents music. They could not accommodate more than two days maximum. So, another taxi to Southwark Cathedral. The Bishop, Mervyn Stockwood, was quite theatrical and certainly Anglo-Catholic it seemed to me coming from an Evangelical school. I had met him as a senior boy sent there on a weekend retreat from my boarding school, Monkton Combe, outside Bath.

At Southwark, a row of clergy in blue-grey cassocks skipped up to Konrad Swinarski and me and I thought perhaps we had found the place! Also, we had Monday to Friday inclusive. It proved a rave and the demand could easily have taken another week or more. It really was an amazing experience. It seemed as if all the Polish Londoners came and plenty of non-Polish Londoners too. Even Nureyev contacted me and came. He had to see this rave in London. I really got the idea from going to see Benjamin Britten's church opera, 'Burning Fiery Furnace', with The English Opera Group. I wish there was time to write more about this week at Southwark Cathedral. I picked the technical staff who I had worked with in the World Theatre Season - rogues, gypsies and vagabonds. I phoned Stratford for a supply of production rough habits for the so-called front-of-house staff and ticket sellers, so all seemed part of the story. Konrad was thrilled with the British response. The last night was quite crazy, with vodka tots going around regularly and the organ being loudly played by Phillip Hoare, who acted as Stage Manager. Yes, very exciting. This was followed to end the season with a young Ugandan dancing and singing group consisting of fine young men and women from Kampala. Most had been in Catholic schools and others from Anglican ones. Most of them had at least one parent who had been murdered by Idi Amin on the rampage against Christianity. And so that ended this mini-season and the World Theatre Season altogether. Robert Serumaga, the Director of this little troupe, asked me if I would be their manager. Now, this was not something that had crossed my mind. Trying to be helpful, I suggested contacting somebody in Warsaw at Pagart, the equivalent of the Arts Council, which was about to open a Festival and might have some spaces to fill, though I thought it most unlikely. Much to my surprise, Masza said yes, she had some space but "only if David Rees will manage you in and around Poland." I had had such happy dealings with Masza and the Polish companies during the World Theatre Seasons and, as I had nothing else on the horizon, I said yes. I contacted Caroline Daubeny, their daughter, asking if she wanted to be involved in something mad and to join on a project basis which she did. Earlier in the year, Molly, her mother, had asked if I would be happy for her to be my secretary for the mini WTS season. I could hardly say no. She was a great backup to me and popular with the Aldwych staff. Above all, she was most efficient. So, she remained in London whilst I went off to Poland. She had agreed to manage the Ugandans around Italy, a trip that followed Poland, whilst I was in London setting up the Round House gig.

In the winter/spring of 1976, I joined up with the charismatic Black American dancer, William Luther, in Cardiff. He was director of the small group of dancers in the Welsh Dance Company. Bill was from the Martha Graham School and her Company. Unfortunately, the Welsh Arts Council were terminating their subsidy, so really, I was the undertaker! However, for the final period of life, I had found some dates in Scotland for both performances and some educational sessions. Bill was a fun person to be with. Whilst in Cardiff, we had some jolly dinners together. On Friday afternoons, we would rush to catch the train back to London. Whilst in Scotland, I tried to negotiate a way of switching Bill and his group of dancers with the help of Tim Dalton, the Director of Dance and Drama at the Scottish Arts Council, and set them up in Aberdeen with the possible help of US funding through the oil. These were the early and successful days of the oil refineries in the North Sea. Of course, this was the plan Tim and I had in mind. Scottish Ballet was already well established in Glasgow. However, Bill did not respond to the idea unless I was willing to join him. He really wanted to return to London and dance. So, the plan was not pursued further. Those youthful dancers - whatever happened to them, I wonder? John Field had taken over as Director of the Royal Academy of Dancing, having left La Scala Milan as Director of Ballet. I joined him as Administrator. The Academy, with its fine premises in Battersea, was very close to my flat - within walking distance. At first, I found the whole set-up very strange and far removed from the world of the theatre. However, I did become keenly interested in the new Professional Dancing Teaching Course, particularly as dancers I knew from the Royal Ballet were on the course. The other interest for me was dealing with the revising of the Royal Charter and that world I had hardly heard about before. I only stayed with the RAD for about 18 months as I was appointed Administrative Director of the London Festival Ballet to work with and support Beryl Grey, the Artistic Director.

During the autumn of 1977, I would go once a week to meet with the retiring Administrative Director Paul Findley, sometimes joined by the Finance Director Peter Morris. I joined the London Festival Ballet at New Year with the Company at the Royal Festival Hall with the annual season of 'Nutcracker' in full swing. Whilst I had seen several performances of the ballet over the years, it was a ballet never included in the repertoire of the Royal Ballet Touring Company. In my early days with the Company, it was customary to have two seasons at the Royal Festival Hall over the Christmas and New Year period and in July/August time, usually with triple bill programmes. This was 1978 and the Company were giving a season of Rudolf Nureyev's greatly acclaimed 'Romeo and Juliet', which had premiered at the London Coliseum in 1977, at Palais des Sports in Paris, nightly for 8 weeks. The arena had a seating capacity of around 11,000 so a lot of money was being made. There was quite a syndicate involved, but the Company (LFB) was earning a good sum too, which it desperately needed. Its history was one of constant financial difficulties. I was fortunate that the Company had such a fine Finance Director, Peter Morris. Our Chairman, Gerry Weiss, told me before I officially joined that Peter was in charge of all things financial. Of course, Nureyev was the main attraction in Paris, but the Company also had a great success, although it was a heavy toll on them with no change of programme to triple ballets that would give some relief to the body.

In the first weeks of the season, I would spend the weekends in Paris to share updates with Beryl Grey and catch up on other Company matters. One Sunday, being free, we went to Le Sacre Coeur and lit our two candles. On Monday morning, I returned to London. I was hardly back a full day before the phone rang and it was a call from Heather Knight, Beryl's loyal and competent Personal Assistant, calling me back to Paris. It seemed that during the performance that night before, there had been a fracas between Rudolf and one of Rosaline's friends danced by Liliana Belfiore (known in the Company as Billy Fury). She had gone to Rudolf's dressing room just before the start of the performance saying she would not take a curtain call at the end of the performance. A few obscenities were exchanged. When it came to Act I with Romeo and Rosaline's friend, he kicked her in the posterior; well, certainly touched her with his toe. So now she was going to the Prefecteur in Paris. Beryl and I and Liliana's latest boyfriend were trying to persuade her otherwise - to and fro. After curtain calls were over, I took Rudolf back to his dressing room and sat alongside him, both of us looking at each other in the mirror. Beryl came in and joined us. Of course, she had had difficulties with him already so was fraught over this latest situation. She said, "Rudolf, there's nothing right with my dancers, with my orchestra or with my staff." Mercifully, Rudolf's masseur, Luigi, was close at hand as I was to Beryl. Rudolf went berserk, picked up a massive brass candlestick to the left of him and aimed it at Beryl. Luigi grabbed Rudolf and I pulled Beryl to the right. It sounds like a real farce, but it could have been otherwise. The parties separated. So next, we had to dissuade the Argentinian from going to the Prefecteur before Paris had a story. The latest boyfriend comforted her so that was finally solved. Beryl and I returned to our hotel, by now in the early hours, to some unappetising sandwiches.

The next day was spent trying to pick up the pieces and I returned to London and then back to Paris at the end of the week for a meeting with Sandor Gorlinsky, the very powerful agent for Rudolf, Callas, Makarova and other international mega artists. He knew I was new to the scene so expected I would be a walk-over. Before we went into the meeting, I said to Beryl to say nothing for she was the "wounded lady". Sandor - not that we were on first-name terms at this stage - said that Miss Grey was not to talk to or have any contact with Rudolf. I replied she was unlikely to want to. Before going into the meeting, I had arranged with the Company Manager that if I was not out of there within 20 minutes, to knock on the door and say my international call had come through. I later told Beryl that we must discuss the situation as, fortunately, the contract for the summer visit of 2 weeks with Rudolf at the Metropolitan in New York, followed by 9 weeks with Nederlander around the US West coast with just 'Romeo and Juliet' would have to be reviewed. Yes, we must make it work in New York at the Metropolitan House, but to tour around the USA with just 'Romeo and Juliet' after this Paris experience would be very questionable.

Yes - Rudolf Nureyev is a phenomenon capable of being a monster too, especially when he may be under any stress. I had learnt earlier that one never should say no to him otherwise one had lost the battle even before discussing the problem. I think he had too many 'Niets' as a boy and as a teenager in the Soviet Union days. The next day, I "ferried" back to London. Before leaving Paris, Beryl said, "Perhaps we should not have lit those two candles in Le Sacre Coeur!"

Once back in London, I discussed with Peter Morris, the Finance Director, what we had forfeited in income during the Summer Royal Festival Hall season in order to fulfil the income that would be earned from the 9 weeks around the USA West Coast. This would be noticeably more though there was quite a syndicate involved who would have to have their cut. I discussed with George Mann, Director of the RFH, how many days we could reclaim for LFB. I think he said he could give us 12 or 14 days which he would pencil in and hold for us, but I must confirm in the next couple of days. He reminded me that the powerful impresario in London - chiefly for music and international artists - Victor Hochhauser, had already booked the other dates for when he would be returning to LFB. Then I contacted Jane Hermann who was Director of the Nureyev Dance season in June/July 1978 with LFB at the Metropolitan House. I arranged that she and I should meet to discuss the rearranging of the contract. On the draft contract, which my predecessor had left for me to sign, to my horror, I had seen that LFB was in tiny print at the bottom of the page. So, I moved it to the top of the page immediately below RN in a slightly smaller print size. But this could not happen until Beryl was back in London to agree with me on these changes. Not surprisingly, around the London dance world, the Company was being called "rent a corps"! "The Mafia" were waiting for me to return with the signed contract and Gorlinsky was expecting me to discuss it at his hotel on that last Saturday of the season. The bleak day came. Beryl and Peter Hulme, the Company Manager, met me at the airport. I said I needed a whisky on our way to Georges Cinque Hotel. I drank my whisky and was ready to leave when Beryl said to Peter, "Give David another whisky," but I declined, so off we went to the lion's den. Gorlinsky arrived in his Astrakhan-collared overcoat smoking a cigar and emitting brandy fumes. Once in his salon, he said, "Now, about the Rudolf US tour of the West Coast arranged by Nederlander management." I replied, "What tour? We will come to New York but are not on the West Coast tour. " He was aghast and speechless. Then he spluttered, "You are totally irresponsible; your administration is hopeless". I replied, "Well, Mr Gorlinsky, I expected you to say something like that." This tirade continued for a while until I rose to my full short height and said, "Beryl, I can see we are wasting Mr Gorlinsky's and our own time, so we should leave." And so, we did. We had both planned that I would not come back for the last night and then Beryl could say that without David being present, the contract could not be signed.

The day before I was back in London, I had a call from Sven, her husband, saying that Beryl was greatly stressed (in so many words) and that she needed me beside her. So, off I went to Paris again for the last time. I knew he would be grouping with the international parties connected to the Metropolitan visit and follow-on tour on the West Coast. I knew he was forever trying to catch me at the Company hotel, so I had my telephone number blocked by Reception. We decided to both return to London and to leave from the back entrance of the hotel via the kitchens in the basement. Peter Hulme, the Company Manager, drove us to the Gare du Nord to catch the boat train for Boulogne and ferry across the Channel. The Eurostar had not yet been completed.

I then met Jane Hermann at the Savoy Hotel. We signed the revised contract. I was half expecting to be sacked. Very soon afterwards, the Company left on its Winter Regional tour. Unlike the Royal Ballet's 12 weeks around the UK Regions, the Festival Ballet were committed to just four-week tours. When touring, I would join the Company for just the Monday night as we had a Company Manager on the road as I had been with the Royal on tour. Before reaching June, the Technical Director was concerned about the shipping of all the 'Romeo and Juliet' set to New York as Rudolf would not accept any changes to the set and the production must be seen as it was the previous year at the London Coliseum where it had been a triumph. So, David asked if I would chair a meeting with Rudolf, David, etc., plus the Coliseum Technical Director who I felt Rudolf would find pleasing to the eye. As 'Romeo' was in the London Coliseum season immediately before flying to New York, there was a problem with Frigerio's large false proscenium arch, and, if there should be any delay due to possible dock strikes, this could affect our opening night in New York. We had a smaller version of the arch for use on the UK Regional tours, and if used for the forthcoming London Coliseum, our shipping problem would be solved and the whole set could be shipped. Knowing "Niet" was fatal to use in any language with Rudolf, after welcoming everyone, I started with, "Now, Rudolf, we seem to have a problem with shipping 'Romeo and Juliet' to New York. I know you want the production to be seen in the forthcoming London Coliseum season exactly as it was seen last year when your production was a total triumph, but - and this is the problem - it's to do with shipping the complete set including Frigerio's large false proscenium arch. You know we have a smaller version for UK touring. Now, if you were to agree that we use this in London just for this time, then our shipping problem would be solved. We all want you to have a huge triumph in New York very soon." He had been looking at me like a cat and said, "Daveed, you are right - you fuck bastard." I replied with a smile, "Oh, Rudolf, I never checked with my parents". With a catlike grin, he said, "You still fuck bastard!"

In no time, the end of June had arrived, and we were off to New York. Gorlinsky had been trying to get me to agree to cover the costs for the designer Frigerio to be in New York to supervise his designs being prepared for the Metropolitan. However, I refused as the Company could not afford such extra costs. The dress rehearsal day came. We were all rather nervous. There was Gorlinsky waiting for me in the stalls. He screamed, "You have sabotaged the season by not allowing Frigerio to be here!" So, I screamed back, "How dare you use the word sabotage! There are three people who have been working to make this season work - Rudolf, Beryl and me - and certainly not you - so never again use the word sabotage!" and I stormed off. Fortunately, Rudolf was calm throughout the Met season without any flare-ups. Before eight the next morning, my bedside phone rang, and it was Gorlinsky. "Sandor here; I am sorry, I owe you an apology for yesterday." From then onwards, I had good relations with Sandor! The opening night was a triumph for Rudolf and, of course, a great introduction for London Festival Ballet in New York. The tension for everybody leading up to the performance created a marvellous electricity throughout the whole Company.

So, back to London and holidays for all of us. Then back to the Regions and Royal Festival Hall for the Christmas and New Year season. Soon afterwards, Ronald Hynd started creating his new ballet 'Rosalinda' (otherwise 'Die Fledermaus') which premiered at the Dominion Theatre in March/April. Meanwhile, as part of the Sino/British Cultural Agreement, London Festival Ballet and the London Symphony Orchestra were to be the first manifestations of the Agreement. This had come about through the removal of the Gang of Four (Madam Chou and her gang). The British Council were part-sponsoring the visit under part-management of the Hochhauser impresariat and me. I had 3 months to find any shortfall. With great advice and support from Lord Chalfont, I found financial sources. I think it was early May when we set off on Yugoslav Airlines from Belgrade to Beijing, stopping at Karachi at around 7 am, stinking hot in the midst of endless sand. On arrival in Beijing, the silence is what struck first with no sound or sight of birds. The hotel had everything needed, with tea forever being refreshed, and most welcome it was. A so-called bar had been set up that seated four people. The wine tasted more like plum juice and there was no spirit on offer. Beer would have been non-alcoholic.

Beryl Grey was already known in the Chinese dance world as she had had great success when she danced there, and she had written of it in "Through

The Bamboo Curtain". The Company opened with 'Giselle' and a triple bill. I remember Peter Schaufuss and Eva Evdokimova as our regular guest artists, and principals Patricia Ruanne, Elisabetta Terabust, Manola Asensio and Liliana Belfiore (Billy Fury). We attended ballet school demonstrations and in one, I remember a child of 12 who danced a solo from 'Don Quixote' and performed amazing feats that left our Principals gasping, wondering how she did it still with the body of a child.

Walking around, I remember seeing the people reading wall newspapers avidly. Of course, since the Gang of Four had been removed, at last, they had achieved so-called freedom. They were still dressed in their cotton suits and caps with a red star above the peak of the cap, but the young people would talk quite freely. They seemed to have two enemies: The Gang of Four and The Russians. One day, we were taken to the Great Wall. I do not remember the dancers coming and they had probably been advised against it, for later in the day, the calves of my legs felt very weak and unhappy! But it had been a real history lesson to walk the Wall of steep inclines, if only to look across to Manchuria.

Everywhere on this trip, wisteria was in full bloom, rich in colour and scent. Of course, all the wisteria in season in the United Kingdom, chiefly in the South of England, originates from China. The Company were offered free acupressure. Most of the dancers, of course, took the opportunity. My therapist was a tiny lady who used silk cloths for silk seemed in abundance. In the next booth to me was one of our hefty technical staff who was yelling and shouting when his therapist touched nerves. I was much relieved by my session. Whilst in Beijing, I would watch people on their lunch break exercising in parks and gardens in what I was calling shadow boxing. However, once back in London, I was told by the Chinese Cultural Councillor and his wife that what I had witnessed was Tai Chi. Since I did suffer acute headaches or possible migraines in those days, his wife offered to teach me some basic Tai Chi, starting with the head. Ever since, I have followed this rule except on Sundays - not for any religious reason.

From Beijing, we flew to Shanghai and more wisteria - not hysteria. Tea was being freshly served but we never saw it being done; we never saw staff around yet knew everything was being serviced. Again, no birds outside. The Chinese are used to protocol. As in Beijing, we were invited to further banquets. I noticed in both cities that the higher echelons in government have far higher-quality dress fabric than the lower realms of society. The material of their smart little suits is finer. However, all Chinese – well, in those days - had a spittoon cup with a cap which they used often during the course of the meal. To us Europeans, we find the custom rather offensive until over the shock. Towards the end of our stay in Shanghai, we were taken for a day trip to Suchow. Quite close by is the most ancient garden in China. It is the rock formations that are so fascinating as if from prehistoric times.

So then back to London. The Nureyev Hochhauser Season at the London Coliseum was, I think, another tour which turned quite ugly. Nureyev's Board supporter was busy trying to activate some dancers to rise against Beryl as Artistic Director. One night, I was obliged to attend a student performance at the Arts Education Institute in the Barbican area along with John Field and his wife, Anna Heaton. When we were leaving, Nureyev's Board supporter insisted on giving me a lift. I said he should drop me off at Knightsbridge as I could get home easily from there to Battersea. Instead, he drove on to his home to a prepared supper. In the process, he gave me a grilling as to why I was not supporting the removal of the Artistic Director. I was so angry and blurted out, "Do you expect me to stab them in the back? I was engaged by the Chairman and the Board to fully support the Artistic Director!" and I rushed out of the house, knowing I had doomed myself further to what had occurred at the end of Paris. And after just a few weeks, Beryl resigned at the end of the Royal Festival Hall season. She left with the huge success of Peter Schaufuss's beautiful production of 'La Sylphide' with Eva Evdokimova which Beryl had asked him to create.

We left for holidays and John Field was confirmed as the new Artistic Director of London Festival Ballet. He joined the Company in November when we were in Bristol mounting Glen Tetley's 'Sphynx' designed by Rouben Ter-Arutunian. Soon, it was back to the RFH for the 'Nutcracker' season. John and I had developed a fine working relationship in the Royal Ballet Touring Company, and a personal friendship with him and his elegant wife Anne Heaton, and again during my brief time with the Royal Academy of Dancing. Now, in Festival Ballet, life is different. We have both been round the block since the RB days. With the London Festival Ballet, you are really alone - "the buck stops there." Unfortunately, I seemed unable to establish that similar communication. I think he thought of me as still a Company Manager rather than Administrative Director. Around this time, within our season at the London Coliseum, the LFB celebrated Bela Bartok's centenary with a double bill of 'The Wooden Prince', a ballet choreographed by Geoffrey Cauley and designed by Philip Prowse and music by Bela Bartok. Both Geoffrey and Philip had last worked together at Covent Garden in John Copley's production of 'Orfeo'. At the Coliseum, the ballet was followed by the opera 'Bluebeard's Castle'. It was an interesting collaboration.

A couple of years after John had joined, at a Board of Governors meeting, the Chairman announced that John was taking over as the Director (Managing Director) of the Company. This was complete news to me. I could see there was really no room for me in the capacity in which I had originally been engaged.

If Peter Daubeny and the World Theatre Seasons had still been alive, I would have tried to return to such happy times. In the early 80s, John mounted a new 'Swan Lake' with designs by Carl Toms. It was a really lavish production and costly. I think it was unjust that John should be responsible for that. I thought his revamping of the choreography for Act 4 was really beautiful.

Just a few years later, Elizabeth Anderton decided to leave after some years of considerable artistic input to LFB. She was, and still is, a fine and distinguished teacher and repetitrice. Later, the dancers discovered and were in consternation. Some came protesting at my door. "You should go to the Director, not me," I said. The following year, John decided he would not extend his contract for another five years. The Board were about to announce that Peter Schaufuss was to take over as Artistic Director. There was already a new Chairman, Sir Ian Hunter. It was leaked to me by the ex-Chairman, Gerry Weiss, that the Board would be axing me at the end of the Season. So off I went into the void again. I had enjoyed my seven years with the Company. Like the Royal Ballet dancers, so the London Festival Ballet dancers and staff were fine people to live and work amidst. And I was fortunate with a loyal colleague, Peter Morris, who was most supportive both professionally and personally.

I saw no place for me in the dance world anymore. It had been a great and exciting time for me, but everything comes to an end, and this required rethinking of one's future still in the Performing Arts. Despite uncertainties, I felt I had gained a kind of liberation. I was now able to be more honest personally. I could feel, think and say whatever without a care. I was free of having to play political games, and frankly, having to handle some folk in power - on Boards - with care. So, I am now a free agent and if I fall flat on my face, only I pay the price. After a good Company send-off with a presentation and dancing in the Royal Festival Hall Ballroom with some of the "kids" following the last performance of the season, for some of the dancers and me, this was the end of our LFB experience. I knew I would miss the dancers most certainly, but life moves and lives and waits - not for those who stop.

Part 5

Next day, I flew to Nice to stay for 10 days with my dear friend Bridget and her husband Jock. They were at the airport to drive to her mother's home in Seillans, a charming village in Provence. After a delightful and relaxing ten days, Bridget and Jock drove me to Nice and, after buying some pizzas for a beach picnic, we drove to catch my boat to Ajaccio to take a bus over the Corsican mountains to the south of the island to Bonifacio. From there, I would take another boat to Santa Maddalena and a taxi to Costa Smeralda close by, the Aga Khan's residence, for Musica in Casa organised by Simonetta Lippi who lived in Rome and who I had met some years earlier in the Spoleto Festival. She was trying to set up her own Festival in Costa Smeralda the following year and wanted me to join her. I heard some lovely music, and ate delightfully prepared pasta and wine, but nothing sensibly developed. So, I returned to London into the void to start again. I knew it would not be with the dance other than as backup.

Just before I left London Festival Ballet, the South Bank Director, newly appointed by the GLC "government" led by Ken Livingston, asked me to a meeting. He wanted to know what my plans were for the future. To be honest, I wished I could tell precisely. However, I told him that I hoped to set up my own small-scale programmes with leading actors and actresses and musicians ranging from classical to jazz, anthologies and cabaret, with leading artists. He suggested seasons at the RFH on Sundays through so many weeks and wanted us to meet again when my plans had developed. In time, that is what happened. The stable of artists and programmes developed mainly by word of mouth from the artists.

Meanwhile, one morning in early December 1984, the phone rang at 7 am. At first, I did not recognize the coughing and spluttering voice of the Goddess of the Dance, Margot Fonteyn. She had just arrived at Heathrow from Panama and wanted to see me. I said something like, "I have plenty of time on my hands". And so, after she had recovered from any jet lag, we met at the Hyde Park Hotel the next day. She had recently learnt from Rudolf that I had left LFB. Panama's little ballet company, Ballet Nacional de Panama, wanted her to take over the Company which already had an existing Artistic Director. She said she would only consider being Artistic Advisor if I came out to conduct a survey of the company and its current structure and give a full report. I already knew that some of the dancers went to Cuba in the summer for classes with the eminent Cuban ballerina and teacher, Alicia Alonso. So, why had the Soviets not forged links by sending one of the great dancers from Leningrad or Moscow? Maybe the Foreign Office in London should be alerted by the British Ambassador in Panama and thereby get some British Council funding for my visit in 1985. So that is what happened for two months from April 1985, right in the change of the two climate seasons.

I arrived on a Saturday and very soon had cramps in my hands and fingers. On arrival, I was contacted by Fred Sill, a typically tall American of Norwegian origin and a friend of Margot's. When I told him about my locked fingers, he said he would get me a supply of salt pills for the next day. So, on Sunday morning, we left for Margot and Tito's home some miles away from Panama City amidst the groves of banana trees leading to the edge of the Pacific Ocean. I learnt from Margot that daily, at around 6 am, she would set off on this walk and splash into the Pacific. In those days, swimming was the one sport ballet dancers could enjoy but not really any other. So, the next day, Fred collected me and off we set, only stopping to collect various ingredients for our lunch, including gin. I had never seen Margot drink gin or any other alcoholic drink in her dancing years. Seeing her in this Panamanian bucolic setting, she looked so relaxed, laughing and smiling. I have heard people in London say that she lived in a tin shed. That is absolute nonsense. Yes, the home was very simple, but the climate does not allow for anything grandiose. Right at this time, we were in the middle-of-season change from dry to wet (or was it the other way?). Certainly, whilst in Panama, I found the wet heat at midday rather trying. Before leaving, Fred and I met Tito in his chair. I, perhaps rather foolishly, tried to shake hands but his upper body felt like touching marble as a result of having been shot in May/June 1964. And it was lead from the bullets poisoning the blood that had paralysed his body. Certainly, one could see Margot's utter peace, calm and strength with Tito. Whilst his speech had been totally damaged, yet Margot understood what he was trying to say. The two loves in her life were Tito and the dance and that is an absolute truth.

Next day, we met at the charming small Italianate Opera House right on the edge of the Pacific. She insisted that the dancers should have one or two performances every week during a season and suggested I should view both front and backstage. Of course, this approach was entirely and rightly based on her own experience at Sadler's Wells. She was quite clear that this is how a ballet audience and following must be built up to support the Panama Ballet Company. She said that I must view the large theatre (2000-seater at least) in the American zone of the Panama Canal where galas could take place with megastars of the time: Nureyev,

Makarova, Baryshnikov and others. It was interesting to hear how and what another real megastar was thinking and saying. Whilst in the American Zone, I also viewed the canal. I think Margot had arranged both visits. From one of the control cabins, I was able to see the raising of one of the large liners, starting with the tip of a huge funnel, into its full grandeur. All it needed was the full pomp and again grandeur of Tchaikovsky's music for the Prologue of 'The Sleeping Beauty'. I had another meeting with Margot on the structure of the company as it would certainly not consist of more than 20 dancers depending finally on how much funding we could secure from the Panamanian Government and commerce. I was loaned an electric typewriter to start my report and proposals sent to Margot for comments would then be submitted to the authorities.

A press conference was arranged by our British Ambassador who was a friend of Margot's. Venturo, a young protégé of both Margot and Tito, was Tito's companion. He carried and lifted Tito into his chair. This particular morning, he arrived with Tito in an anteroom and, unknown to the rest of us, the double doors opened and there was Margot, wheeling in her husband, all smiles, as indeed Aurora appearing in Oliver Messel's archway for her first entrance in 'The Sleeping Beauty Act 1'.

On Sunday evening, I went to Mass at a church not far from my hotel. I noticed a military man walking quite close behind me. I took my place near the back of the church and there was the military man just a few rows behind me again. After the Mass, I set off for my hotel and again the military man was behind me. The streets seemed deserted so I thought I would stop and confront him with why he was following me. He said, "I am protecting you because somebody, who we the military suspect, has been trailing you on this visit." Well, one never knows really what happens in Panamanian politics! Nothing more was heard of the matter. My last day arrived and an open-air party had been arranged at the home of two members of the existing Company, including the Ballet Master, who had been trained at the Royal Ballet School in London. It was a beautiful evening and the climate had settled down. We were all gathered together when Margot arrived with her usual allure, looking so cool (in the original meaning of the word). The dancers were thrilled. One of the boys - I wish I could remember his name – was spotted. Margot nudged me and said, "He could become a fine dancer and has fine presence on stage." I learnt that he went to Cuba for Alicia Alonso's classes in the summer.

Next day, I flew back to London and torrential rain. As I sat in the gloom, a knock on my front door roused me. This was my first meeting with someone to whom I had been chatting frequently. He was delivering his fresh supply of leaflets for the SDP (Social Democratic

Party) that I would circulate in my Battersea area. I was one of the first 100 to join the SDP in the early 1980s. By 1.00 pm, I realised I had made a new friend in him and later, his delightful Russian/French wife Moussia, who was a charming and most imaginative cook and who produced delicious suppers up in their Clapham home.

On Margot's next visit to London, we met to discuss plans for the future now that US Gin Distilleries had agreed to fund the Panama Ballet Company project. She was adamant that I should return to Panama to kickstart my proposals in my survey for the future of the Company, otherwise nothing would happen. I was rather hesitant and told her that I was already trying to set up my own little business as Management Consultant for the Performing Arts with small-scale programmes with leading actors and musicians ranging from classical to jazz. Undaunted, Margot said she could help me get connections in Florida, New York and California who would jump at being associated with artistic projects with especially distinguished artists from London and so create their own Arts Festivals. Sometime later, with my Battersea home almost let for a year by a very upmarket Knightsbridge estate agent contact of Margot's and my flight to Panama booked, I had a frantic call from Margot telling me to cancel the flight as the Gin Distilleries had cancelled their funding. And so, the Panamanian project was off temporarily, however, sadly, this became the permanent outcome. Tito's health was deteriorating, and he died in 1989. Later, Margot was diagnosed with cancer and walking with a stick. She endured such heavy treatment. I used to get quite regular reports from her close TV friend Paddy Foye who knew about the Panamanian project. Paddy had directed 'Magic of the Dance' which Margot had presented - a memorable series. Dear Margot died in February 1991 and Rudolf, The Phenomenon, not so long afterwards.

From this sadness, life goes on, so I must continue developing my stable of programmes and artists. The South Bank offered me the first Autumn series of some of my programmes in 1988. This included 'An Agreeable Blunder', an anthology devised and performed by Janet Suzman, supported by Bill Homewood on guitar and as her cavalier; 'Once Below A Time' - the story of Dylan Thomas's life told in his own words through the stories, poems, letters and drama, by turns hilarious, sublime and tragic, compiled by John Edmunds and presented by him and Rosalind Shanks; 'Lorca', the story of the great Spanish poet, created and performed by Trader Faulkner; 'Sons and Mothers', an anthology devised and performed by Roger Rees and Virginia McKenna, and 'An Anthology of Words and Music', devised by and performed by Ludovic Kennedy and Moira Shearer, with harpist Gillian Tingay. Within this season, through Polish contacts in Warsaw, I was able to present a great chanteuse at the time, Eva Demarczyk, at the Queen Elizabeth Hall. Through this connection, I was able to find one of the greatest Russian artists I have had the privilege to find - Elena Kamburova - a circus clown, a chanteuse, an actress... yes, a great artist who I brought to the QEH during Gorbachev's Perestroika period before there was any influx of Russians other than those who had come to the UK to escape the Soviet Revolution. Elena conquered the house that was essentially a London audience.

During the next few years, I managed to build up my "stable" of artists and programmes substantially to 36 and some of them often directed me to other very distinguished artists, actors and musicians such as the redoubtable solo and tour de force performance of the great American/English actress Irene Worth in her 'Portrait of Edith Wharton'. I remember the first performance I presented in the charming regency theatre in Chipping Norton. The Saturday night was already booked out, chiefly by well-heeled middle-class women. Irene was wearing the original Fortuny gown he had created for Lilian Gish and looking very statuesque. Edith Wharton tells of her unconsummated marriage to a wealthy New York homosexual. Later in her life, having settled in France, she met a Frenchman and she experienced consummation for the first time. Irene delivered this experience brilliantly by pausing, and, with a flourish upwards of her hand, said,

"Speaking from a woman's point of view...." With that, the audience, comprised chiefly of women, rose and applauded, shouting "Bravo!" stamping their feet – this reveals the power of women.

Now, I cannot remember whether it was Christopher Logue, poet and sometime contributor to Private Eye, or the stunning actor Alan Howard who contacted me about again presenting Christopher's 'Kings', "the marvellous rendering of the Iliad" (Observer) which we did at Greenwich, Stratford upon Avon (Swan Theatre) and for 3 weeks at the Tricycle Theatre, Kilburn. After an uncertain first week, it took off like a rocket and could have run for a few more weeks as it showered gold dust. There were several other programmes that glittered: 'Fond and Familiar' with Judi Dench, Michael Williams and John Moffatt, 'My Southern Heart' with the fabulous jazz singer Marion Montgomery, and Laurie Holloway & double bass, Roger Pringle's memorable 'Thomas Hardy – The Man and the Poet' presented by Barbara Leigh Hunt & Richard Pasco, several of John Edmunds' anthology programmes and many more including John Julius Norwich's own anthologies plus his two very fine illustrated talks: 'Venice' and 'Byzantium'. We took all these programmes and others to many festivals around the United Kingdom as well as the Stratford Poetry Festival and the British Library.

One day in the early 1990s, the Director of Sadler's Wells Royal Ballet, later to found and move the

Company to become Birmingham Royal Ballet, (Sir) Peter Wright and I were talking about Dame Ninette de Valois' love of reading. This reminded me of her book of poems, 'Cycle', which I had come across in the Royal Academy of Dancing bookshop around 1977 when I was still the Administrator before moving to the London Festival Ballet. So now, in early 1992, I thought a little programme could be created for limited presentation. This developed into 'Madam's Choice'. I gathered together Rosalind Shanks and Paul Daneman for the original performance, succeeded by John Moffatt and Stephen Lade. It was great fun to put together. I must have told Leslie Edwards, one of Madam's earliest dancers, who told me that I must talk to Graham Bowles, master of English at the Royal Ballet School and a friend of his and Madam's. He then said to me, "Good luck when you go to see Madam about the project!" So, I arrived at the front door of her flat and somebody opened the door. Eventually, Madam came down the dark corridor. She peered at me and said, "I think I know you. So, what do you want to talk to me about?" I said who I was and she replied, "I know that."

"I want to make a small programme that includes some of your poems, favourite writers and music." She replied, "What a ridiculous idea!" I retorted, "I rather expected you to say that Madam," as we went into her sitting room. "A glass of wine?" she asked. "I rarely drink any alcohol at lunchtime nowadays." She gave me a look as if I was some wimp! “Yes, I will, please, if I may.” She dashed behind an open screen and soon produced two glasses of red wine. I sat on the sofa and she in her armchair close at hand. “So, what is this all about?” Now with her glass in hand, she was perfectly relaxed and asked, “Where do we start?” “Madam, all I want from you are names of some of your favourite writers, poets and composers.” She quickly said, “You cannot expect me to choose my own poems from the ‘Cycle’.” “No, I don’t; Rosalind and I will choose those.” She was now most responsive and seemed genuinely interested in the project. She was most interesting and sometimes really emphatic in her personal choice of both writers and music. Obviously, Tchaikovsky was at the top of the list and possibly more highly regarded than Mozart. Of course, WB Yeats was high on the list of writers along with Trollope, Tolstoy, Louis MacNeice and Blake. It proved to be such a rewarding meeting. ‘Madam’s Choice’ owed much of its success to the music linkage provided through Stephen Lade’s creative imagination. Initially, when I asked at the end what was Madam’s favourite musical instrument, suggesting the harp, she replied instantly, “Certainly not,” and added, “the violin”. I replied, “Rather tricky as the violin is so beautiful but also so exposed.” “Yes, of course,” she said. After all, she was well used to the piano. When the Sadler’s Wells Ballet was evacuated during World War II to the Manchester area, Constant Lambert and the Company pianist, the memorable Hilda Gaunt, provided the music on two upright pianos for all performances.

So 'Madam's Choice' was presented for the Friends of Covent Garden on the day Madam received the highest honour from Her Majesty the Queen - the Order of Merit - and came straight from the Palace to the Royal Opera House. Afterwards, Madam met the artists and was very gracious to all four of us. This presentation was given again but now with John Moffatt replacing Paul Daneman in Birmingham to celebrate the very recent knighthood of Sir Peter Wright.

Shortly after the collapse of the USSR, I came across the Konevets Vocal Quartet from St. Petersburg. They had come to Paris and London on a private visit through a Russian/French friend and an English fluent Russian-speaker from Oxford. The singers had met Anne and Catriona at Konevets Monastery, on the vast Lake Ladoga, which had been occupied by the Red Army who had finally advanced to break the interminable and deathly siege of Leningrad (St. Petersburg). After the collapse of the USSR, the Monastery had been returned to the Russian Church and slowly monks were returning too. At this time, the Konevets Quartet were providing the musical liturgy and, as the Community increased, the Quartet were teaching them to sing. Feeling a little fragile on an early November Sunday morning after a late night out, sipping my tea and contemplating whether or not I would make Mass at my local church, meanwhile trying to listen to Michael Kay's choice of music, I heard – yes - this divine Russian liturgical sound and I was resurrected from the night before. Michael Kay explained that these young Russians would be singing on the following Tuesday evening in a City of London church. I checked the number I called which was answered with a very brusque vicar's voice. Come the Tuesday, I cycled from Battersea in the fog to Bank close to the Mansion House. There were about 12 people in the very front of the nave who proved to be old Russian émigrés. I stayed at the back waiting. These young Russians came and stood in front of the altar. There was silence and then arose this amazing and sublime sound that transcended everything. There was a short break when the young woman, Catriona Bass from Oxford, was selling the one and only cassette tape of their liturgical music. The upshot of this was that Catriona arranged for me to meet Igor Dmitriev, the bass and founder/director of the quartet the next day.

We met in a café next door to the Coliseum Theatre. I told him he should be taking the Konevets Quartet to Festivals around the United Kingdom. His reply, with his basso profundo voice - "Please, you take us." I really had not thought of this. However, I agreed to consider the possibility of setting up a short tour in the south and another in London in early September 1994, and I set this up on a shoestring financially. We had amazing concerts that attracted so many. This led to several years of concerts around the United Kingdom. Whilst I had toured around with the Royal Ballet, now, with Konevets Quartet, we concentrated on churches and monasteries which provided the most suitable acoustics. I was taking the Quartet to so many interesting rural scenes and stately homes around the United Kingdom. After a two years touring around the UK, in the autumn of 1996, through various connections, I took the Quartet to the USA, a tour that proved a huge success. We would rent a vehicle and Igor would drive - the most competent and reliable driver. Most Americans were so kind to the Quartet on this tour and all the subsequent tours over the next years across the States and Canada. Many of the concerts were in various churches, including Russian Orthodox, where big lunches and wine were lavished on the "Boys". The Quartet would then sing old Russian imperial and folk songs - nothing from Communist times. I had encouraged them to have appropriate encores both in the UK and USA. Artur, known affectionately as Arturchik, was a jazz singer as well as being a trained Russian liturgical and classical singer. So, for the first West Coast tour, Artur arranged a jazz-style 'Hello Dolly'. It was first sung in San Francisco and received with ecstatic encores except for a few boos which proved to be coming from an anti-Jewish section of the audience who obviously objected to the heroine of the audience, Dolly, being Jewish!

Well, you cannot please everyone. For the UK - just in England, we managed to get a somewhat jazzed-up version of Vera Lynn's 'We'll Meet Again ...' adored by the English naturally.

These years across the Big Pond were great fun as we drove around this vast country other than when distances necessitated flights. The kind of life I was experiencing reminded me of my two years of National Service. For these four had served two years in the Red Army in our equivalent of the Band Boys. They were posted mostly in East Germany and the Baltic and seemed to me to have had quite a cosy time. We were never in the US or Canada during winter, but usually in the Fall, and, when in the New England area, there were the most stunning autumn colours, similar to what would be in Russia and around St. Petersburg. I had been greatly helped by Bob Mitchell and his wife Jo Dare in bringing the Quartet to New York. Being a Trustee of the House of the Redeemer, just off 5th Avenue and with Central Park close by, Bob arranged for the five of us to stay as guests. It was also just up the road from the Metropolitan Museum and the Guggenheim Gallery. We had a few concerts in the Mitchells' local Episcopalian church. Further up and off 5th Avenue was the Russian St Nicholai Church where the Boys sang at the Divine Liturgy, after which we were ferried off for lunch at the Russians' premises. There was certainly no stinting on food or vodka glasses. There, I met a most interesting lady, a secretary in the Russian section of the United Nations. She invited the Quartet and me there on the following day. I accepted instantly. When it came to Monday, the "Boys - Malchiki" were still sleeping. At the time I arrived, Kofi Annan was chairing the meeting between Arafat and Rabin. After that, my Russian friend suggested I might like to see some UN items stored but not being exhibited. What I did see were remnants from Hiroshima. Apart from clumps of rock so pulverised as if they had come from Mars or some other planet, the other outstanding item was a complete statue of Christ minus one uplifted hand and finger - the only non-pulverised remains of the church! One afternoon at this time, another friend acquired from the St. Nicholai lunch who was one of the singers in the church, took us to an enormous hilly cemetery outside New York because it was the anniversary of Sergei Rachmaninov's death. I am a passionate lover of Rachmaninov music. Igor had prepared his own shortened Requiem for Sergei's wife and daughter at the graveside. Igor had trained me to try to sing the 2nd Tenor role. I have a photo of us on my sitting room mirror!

On another visit back to the East Side in New York, Konevets and I drove to Stockbridge, Massachusetts where Bob and Jo Dare had their weekend escape cottage. The Boys gave a Sunday concert in the local Episcopalian church. We had real delicious Jo Dare home cooking. I think at the time she was a senior executive in one of the main Manhattan banks. On the Monday, Bob drove me to see Edith Wharton's chateau which was looking very sad and decaying rather fast. Fortunately, I have recently learnt that it has been completely restored and is being used for suitable purposes. Also, we went to Tanglewood. I do wish I had managed to attend a concert, particularly with a Stravinsky programme and perhaps conducted by Bernstein.

However, those days in the USA with Konevets are over. Why? We may well ask but all of us know why.

Before going to Russia to visit Konevets and their families, I went to Paris for their concert in La Sainte Chapelle with a perfect acoustic. I had already alerted Nina Soufi, sister-in-law of the internationally famous Theatre Director, Peter Brook, about the concert. He did attend with an entourage including a very tall and elegant Russian Orthodox priest. At the end of the concert, he congratulated the Quartet and offered them three concerts at his Bouffes du Nord theatre. Following the concert in La Sainte Chapelle, he wrote a glowing critique in Le Figaro which I have frequently quoted in tour publicity around the world:

"At first, silence - pure silence - and we wait. Miracle: sound of equal purity. Four disembodied voices creating notes that seem to emanate from elsewhere. The small group of young singers from

St. Petersburg, lead us to a space where sound and silence unite."
Peter Brook - Director - Les Bouffes du Nord, Paris

1996 was my first visit to the "Boys" in Russia – yes, to the amazing St. Petersburg. Sadly, a big part of my heart remains there, as do some of my very best friends despite the current situation. Previous to this moment, I had last been in Leningrad in June 1961! Then I was asked if I was Jewish because of my nose and red hair. The former remains, less so the hair! Yes, I am still here! We went to stay at Konevets Monastery on the island of the same name on the great Lake Ladoga from where the Soviet tanks came to break the Nazi siege of Leningrad. This visit was a great experience other than being eaten alive by the whopper mosquitos. A tight sunhat is no obstacle to these monsters. So, thereafter, I changed to early autumn to also get the stunning and majestic autumn colours. I met my friends from Paris, Anne and Edith, with young Cyrille. We all stayed at the Monastery. Nikita and I made our own separate bathrooms in Lake Ladoga. One gets used to ankles that might never be defrosted. Amazing what one can tolerate. On later visits, I stayed with Nikita and Irina in the heart of St. Petersburg. Oh, so many happy memories. I remember, on a later visit to the Monastery, young Father Antonin came around in his pony and trap to take the young children and me around the island going in and out of the tall trees and to see the sparkling lake - magical. In the earlier visits, I recall friendly young Evgeny, one of the monks, smoking fish from the lake for an upcoming meal. He was also baking bread - and most tasty bread too. Later, on a return visit, with Nikita and Irina we visited the now Fr. (Otez) and his wife in his wooden church.

I have certainly had two birthdays among my Russian friends and always an Irina menu of chicken pie with such delicate pastry. I think that Russian women must be the best pastry cooks in all the world. Of course, all this is accompanied by very good vodka straight out of the deep freeze in delicate small glasses unaccompanied by ANY other fluid. That would completely adulterate the purity of the vodka. You might be misled by some rogue giving you the roughest vodka that could painfully kill you! I finished my time and part of my life with Konevets Quartet by taking them to Istanbul in 2010 where they and I had a glorious time around the city and up the Bosphorus. Istanbul is an exciting city where I had previously also been in ballet days in the Istanbul Festival. The food is excellent, especially roasted lamb. Aubergines are prepared and served in such a simple and special way. After Istanbul, I handed the management over completely to Igor Dmitriev, my good friend from past days. When back in London, I decided I would now retire. It was time to explore other parts of life like silence, stillness and its contemplativeness leading to a harmony of being. No, not negativity; hopefully, rather a conclusion. Now I would be free to attend concerts, visit galleries, exhibitions and go to the theatre. Time passed quickly and suddenly, 2016 arrived and I became politically more involved than at any previous time. In the early 80s, I had supported the Gang of Four of Roy Jenkins, Dr David Owen, Shirley Williams and Bill Rodgers who formed the Social Democratic Party, then, in the break away from the Labour Party some years later, they joined the Liberals and become the Liberal Democrats. I was so outraged at the result of Brexit. We had returned to the result of the Reformation but without the religion and certainly insular. A few years later, somebody, obviously a Brexiteer, asked me, "David, what are you... where are you in this charade?" I replied, "Yes, one could call this a charade if it were not so serious. I stand firmly first and foremost as a European, British, an adopted Londoner and Welsh" (completely by blood). And this amalgam I will remain to my last breath.

We have come through Covid, hopefully, as long as we retain some caution. The medical profession has behaved heroically in all aspects and continues to do so. Young folk, by and large, are kind and attentive on transport to older folk.

We lost our much-loved Monarch without any fuss, a queen who had served her country and people with such dignified humility and simplicity. And she has been succeeded by a caring son who seems to be shaping his reign wisely, striving to understand both his country and his people. And he has an equally wise consort. Quite a balancing act for both of them. In the wings is the young couple, again, wisely in attendance. Let us hope our governments can lead the country wisely and free of partisanship and popularism and ego power as the country has had to endure in recent times. These are just some comments and observations of a Commoner, as I continue on this journey. Alas, I have one real sadness - that Russia and my friends are now beyond my reach - though not in spirit. But here I am in Wapping, beside Old Father Thames, perfectly contented. And what one learns is that contentment and harmony in one's own being must be sought - a precious prize - and then moments of happiness descend as moments of bliss. To expect more and consider it one's right will lead to disappointment and unhappiness. We really should know after all these centuries, but as Marlene sings to us still, "When will they ever learn?" And she will be joined by my dear friend, Joseph Markovitch, who really started me off on this spiral. To you, Joseph, my greatest thanks.

For Joseph, from David

Printed in Great Britain
by Amazon